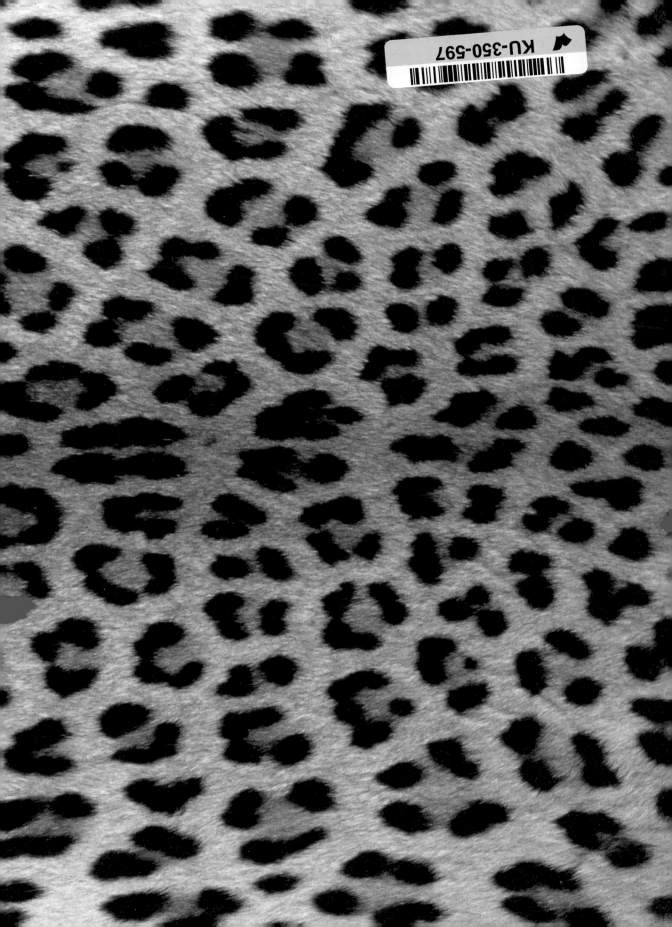

a sort of
A-Z-thing

LILY

With photographs of
Ms Savage by Nicky Johnston

First published in 1998
by HEADLINE BOOK
PUBLISHING

10 9 8 7 6 5 4 3 2 1

Cataloguing in Publication
Data is available from the
British Library

ISBN 0 7472 2300 9

Designed by Roggio Armond

Printed and bound in Great
Britain by Butler & Tanner
Ltd, Frome and London

HEADLINE BOOK
PUBLISHING
A division of Hodder
Headline PLC
338 Euston Road
London NW1 3BH

Picture credits:
Photographs of Ms Savage
by Nicky Johnston except
p2-3, 5 Steve Finn © Alpha;
p10 © BBC; p15 © Graham
Trott; p29, 38, 106 PA News;
p29 © Verne, © M. Harris
Houses and Interiors; p38,
43, 73, 97, 100, 122, 126,
128, 129, 143 Rex Features;
p44-5, 49, 52 National Trust
Photographic Library; p60,
67 © MSI; p68 © Hulton
Deutsch; p79 © Magnum;
p94, 119, 122, 130 ©
Popperfoto; p99 © Hulton
Getty; p10, 13, 16, 18, 21,
23, 26, 27, 28, 72, 73, 74-5,
78, 88-9, 92, 98, 112, 120 1,
123, 132-3 © Justin R
Canning.

Illustration credits: p22, 61,
90 Mike Strudwick, Black
Hat; p24-5, 69, 101, 124,
127, Hussein Hussein; p31-
35, Graham Redfern; p44-
57, 104-5, 109-115, Chris
Lloyd; p10, p12-16, p60,
p63, p64, p69, p72, p136-
141, Brenda Cheape.

DEDICATION

I dedicate this book to the memory of all the feisty showgirls and burleycue queens I've worked and drank with who've gone to that Illuminated Runway of Joy in the Sky.

Thank you.

Introduction

I T WAS MY CLOSE PAL JACKIE COLLINS who first encouraged me to put pen to paper. She was in the middle of writing the sensational *Hollywood Kids* when she was stricken with a temporary bout of writers' block, not something that the prolific J.C. was used to experiencing. I took her to lunch at the 'Belle of Bombay' – There's nothing like a pint of lager and a curry to jog the little grey cells. We chatted for hours. Maybe I gave Jackie some inspiration because she went straight home and finished the book! Of course when I read it I recognised immediately who the character of the Hollywood Madame, Cheryl Landers, was based on! Of course, I didn't mind - anything to help a chum out.

'You should write a book yourself,' she said to me during one of our many transatlantic phone calls.

'Me?' I'd say. 'What would I have to write about? A simple gal with no education from the back streets of Birkenhead? Nonsense.' How was I to know that, under the pen name of Lilian Blythwood, I would eventually write over 46 romantic, historical novels and a gardening manual?

I'm currently writing my memoirs, to be published in six volumes as a boxed set sometime in the next year. It's hard work researching the family tree, so as a break from combing the dusty vaults of the Savage Family I put my memoirs aside and wrote my 'A to Z'. Why call it an *A Sort of A to Z Thing*?, I hear you ask, dear readers - because I couldn't think of a title if you must know! If I were Julie Goodyear I could have called it *Julie's Alpha-Bet* - a clever way of paying reference to the barmaid Bet Lynch she used to play in Coronation Street. But since regrettably my name is not Goodyear, I opted for *A Sort of A to Z Thing*, and it is! A potpourri of fascinating figures and facts, an almanac of sound and sensible advice, everything you ever wanted to know is in these pages. My personal thoughts and feelings, shocking revelations about my family, it's all here.

I've learned a few tricks of the trade on my journey down life's perilous highway. I'm passing them on. Who knows - maybe they can help you?

Whatever you think, thank you for buying it - if you didn't buy it but shoplifted it then a dreadful curse will fall upon your miserable head!

Best wishes
lily x

AGONY AUNT

More people write to me for advice than they do to Denise Robertson on Richard and Judy. Some weeks she doesn't get any letters at all, so I have to bung her a sack of mine to make it look like she's busy. Poor unfortunate souls from all over the globe write to me with their problems, vulnerable, confused men and women seeking my wisdom. It's a bloody nuisance being known as 'The Biggest Heart in Birkenhead'.

Here's a few samples from my mail bag:

Dear Lily,
I've got a terrible crush on the well-known comedian Bernard Manning. Is this wrong?
Doreen

Dear Doreen,
Yes, I'm afraid you are wrong. Bernard Manning is neither well known nor a comedian. Buy yourself an industrial tub of lard and leave it in the sun for a few weeks till it goes a bit smelly, and then pop it in your bed! It makes an ideal Manning substitute.
Yours,
Lily

Dear Lily,
Every time I make love to a woman she just lies there cold, unresponsive and emotionless.
How can I find a warm, responsive woman?
Derek

Dear Derek,
Try making love to a live one.
Yours,
Lily

Dear Miss Savage,
My wife refuses to participate in oral sex, no matter how much I beg her. She keeps her mouth firmly closed. How can I make her change her mind?
Frustrated, Peckham

Dear Frustrated,
Offer her money. If this fails then maybe your personal hygiene leaves a lot to be desired. Give your bits a rinse under the tap. That might tip the balance in your favour.
Yours,
Lily

Dear Lily,
I'm sixteen and still a virgin. A man at the office I work in is very friendly with me. He keeps saying that he's got something that will drive me insane. What is it?
Alice

Dear Alice,
It's probably rabies love, so keep yourself nice. Don't go giving your florin away to a bloody clerical assistant. Hang on to it for someone in a higher position.
Yours,
Lily

Dear Lil,
I never know what to do after I've had sex. Is there a correct procedure? Do I share a cigarette? Go to the bathroom? Offer my partner seconds? What do you do?
Josie, Rhyl

Dear Josie,
I get dressed and go home.
Yours,
Lily

Dear Lily,
I've been married to a pig of a man for the last five years. He's never done a day's work in his life and what little money I bring home from my six cleaning jobs, he drinks.
And when he's drunk he's violent – he comes home from the pub every night and batters me. What can I do? I don't want to leave him as I still love him.
Demented

Dear Demented,

Of course you love him, and to prove your love you must get him off the drink and make him understand that violence is not going to get his tea made any quicker. So, next time he comes home drunk and lays into you, wait until he has gone to bed and is passed out unconscious, and then take action. Buy a baseball bat from any leading sports shop and break every bone in the bastard's body. That'll learn him. Of course he will have to go into hospital, but at least you'll know where he is and he certainly won't be on the ale and taking a swing at you anymore. And you'll have taught him a lesson. You'll probably be able to feed him grapes since he'll be in plaster and on traction. Who knows – it may bring you closer together.

Good luck.

Yours,

Lily

SIX MONTHS LATER I RECEIVED THE FOLLOWING LETTER.

HM Prison Holloway
Prisoner 4129617
Dear Lily,
You and your crappy advice. I bought myself a baseball bat and did what you suggested. I gave him a good hiding. He died in an ambulance and I got life for manslaughter. Any more bright ideas?

There's no point in replying to this sort of letter. I didn't suggest that she kill him, just give him a few playful taps, so it's nothing to do with me. However, I do feel sorry for this poor woman languishing in Holloway, so I've sent her a copy of my book *Coping With Solitary Confinement*, and an autographed photo of myself to stick on her cell wall. That should cheer her up.

Dear Miss Savage,
I am a young farmer living in an isolated part of Ireland. I'm tall, muscular, have black hair and I've been told that I look like Stuart Damon from The Champions. *My problem is a delicate one. Every time I get the chance out here to meet a girl I scare them off. We always get on very well at first but then when it comes to the bedroom they run a mile. You see, how can I put this? I have a very large appendage – it's over a foot long, and all the lasses I've met refuse to have sex with me. How will I ever meet a girl who will let me make love to her?*
Yours,
Sean O'Donnell

Dear Sean,

I'm on me way, and call me Lily.

Yours,

Lily

Dear Lil,

Hi there, pussycat. I've always been a lady-killer, Lil. I've enclosed a photo for you to drool over. Do you think that as I get older I might start to lose my looks?

See ya around,

Phil

Dear Phil,

You will if you're lucky. And call me Miss Savage.

Dear Lily,

I've always been used to the good things in life. My parents are extremely wealthy. I went to all the best girls' schools. I finished my education in Paris and then at my first debs' ball I fell in love ... with a waiter. I realise now it was a stupid infatuation. The man is an idiot. He works 15 hours a day while I have to sit at home bored and he earns no more than £60 a week. How can he provide for me on such a pitiful wage?! My parents have disowned me and my friends avoid me. Was I mad to marry this stupid little loser?

Caroline Steenman Kypriano

Dear C.S.K,

I think he was even madder to propose. Ever heard of getting OFF YOUR FAT ARSE and getting a job?

Lily

Dear Lily,

My boyfriend wants us to have sex in all sorts of different positions. I'm like a contortionist. He's suggested we do it doggie fashion. What do you think?

Doreen

Dear Do,

You put your paw down, love. Keep your back against the mattress – do you really want to make love in the street? Imagine the neighbours! Tell your young man to SOD OFF.

Lily

Dear Lily,

Some of these youngsters today make me sick. They have no respect for the sacred vows of marriage. I've been married for 30 years – to a pig of a man. But even though I hate the sight of him I would never get divorced. I'm totally against it. Why should these girls of today get off what I've had to put up with for the last 30 years?

Yours,

Edna Quinn

Dear Edna,

You should've murdered him on your wedding night – you'd be out now with time off for good behaviour.

AVENGERS

Brilliant tv series, crap movie. Why did they bother making it? Uma who? Uma Thurman? What kind of name is that for a Hollywood star? It sounds like a brand name for loft insulation. I would've made a better Emma Peel than her. I can fill a leather catsuit better than she can. That's if her fighting gear was leather – it looked more like a cheap bit of leatherette from the market to me. I've seen better examples of leather hanging over our window cleaner's bucket. That job should've been mine, but the producers opted for Uma. Men, they always go for the obvious.

I wanted to marry a man like Steed when I was a girl: suave, sophisticated, elegant and who looked fabulous in a bowler hat – more than I can say for Ralph Fiennes who looked

more like the kids' cartoon character Mr Ben than John Steed.

The best Avenger girl without doubt was Linda Thorson as Tara King. Now she could fight. She'd be very handy on a pub crawl around Newcastle.

ACAPULCO

Call me old-fashioned but I always think that if you're gonna get up and sing in public then it's best to a have a bit of music behind you. Even a harmonica or a pair of spoons is preferable to nothing. This Acapulco singing has become very popular particularly at charity benefits for miners and Bosnian refugees. You can bet your last ciggie you'll find a bunch of scruffy women, god help 'em, caterwauling 'Trains and Boats and Planes' in a four-part harmony. If you're lucky, one of them might be banging a tambourine but it's not enough to set your foot tapping. So if you get the urge to sing on stage don't even bother unless you've got a band behind you.

Beauty

THE HOUSE OF SAVAGE™ has been creating beautiful women for over a decade. By that I do not mean that we at the HOUSE OF SAVAGE™ rob graves and then try to bring the rotting corpses to life by means of an electrical storm. We have more accessible ways of rejuvenating human tissue.

Our own personal beauty range – FLAME OF LLANDUDNO™, internationally renowned in all the great beauty houses of the world – is used by film stars, models, royalty and ugly old dogs alike. Whilst we can't profess to be able to make a silk purse out of a sow's ear, our exclusive range of skin care products has made a remarkable difference to the skin of women everywhere.

FLAME OF LLANDUDNO™ is available everywhere to women with more money than sense.

FLAME OF LLANDUDNO™: it's every woman's right to have an immaculate complexion.

THE HOUSE OF SAVAGE™ Skin Rejuvenation Clinic has a reputation for achieving results. Sun-damaged, wrinkled and lined skin will be transformed to its youthful bloom again once our powerful lasers and acid peels get to work.

We believe that by getting right down to the lower dermis of the skin and nourishing the new cells with our secret ingredient we can restore sagging tired skin to its former glory.

The House of Savage is delighted to introduce their exciting new fragrance

VENOM

From a recipe as old as the mists of time, we at the House of Savage have created the smell that spells

'WOMAN'.

Strong and heady, this cloying perfume will linger in any room you've been in for about 10 days after you've gone.

The sweet smell of venom is not something that's easily forgotten. The powerful scent of tuberose combined with musk will catch in his throat and intoxicate his senses.

NOT TO BE TAKEN INTERNALLY. FOR EXTERNAL USE ONLY.

Cellulite is quickly banished at The H.O.S.S.R.C. One plunge in our acid bath and that unsightly flesh just falls off you!

At the moment there is a three-year waiting list with one of our skin specialists but if you bung us a substantial backhander we will see to it that you jump the queue.

And now for the first time THE HOUSE OF SAVAGE™ reveals some of the tricks of the beauty trade.

EYES

Are your eyes like pissholes in snow? Well if you've had a late night drinking or crying hysterically because your husband ran off with another woman and those eyes of yours are a puffy, swollen mess then these top tips will help disguise and repair the damage.

- **Lie down and relax for 15 minutes with two used tea bags over each eye. Not a good idea to lift them straight from the mug – let them cool first.**
- Cucumber slices are the little miracle workers when it comes to reducing puffy eyes. Place a few juicy slices over each eye for 15 minutes, you can use them later in a salad – waste not, want not.
- **Eyebright is a herb that works magic on swollen red eyes. Place four tblsp of dried Eyebright in a teapot and add boiling water. Leave to steep and when the mixture has cooled strain into a bottle and refrigerate. Soak a couple of cotton pads and place over each eye for 15 minutes – you'll be amazed at the results.**

BAGS

If you make Aspel look like he's had a good night's sleep then it's time to get the haemorrhoid cream out. A closely guarded trade secret of top make-up artists, haemorrhoid cream does to bags under the eyes what it does for haemorrhoids – shrinks and tightens 'em!

- **Just dab a small amount under each eye, allow to dry and then apply a concealer – the bags vanish. Not recommended over a long period of time, as the cream will eventually damage the delicate tissue around the eye area causing wrinkles as well as bags. If your bags are here to stay the only way to shift 'em is be going under the knife.**
- Use a haemorrhoid cream such as Preparation H – a suppository will not have the same effect. You can also tighten up those jowls as well, just rub a small amount into the jawline.

EYEDROPS

- **If you're putting drops that have a blue tint into your eye then be careful it doesn't run down your cheeks. Wipe any spillage up immediately as this stuff glows when under a fluoro-light – such as a disco. You want to look like an extra in 'Thriller'? Course not, get it wiped.**

MAKING THE EYE UP

- **A blue eyeliner applied just inside your lower lid, (don't poke your eye out) will make the whites of your eyes look brighter.**
- Eyeliner should only be applied if the hand is steady. Forget it if you have the DTs or are in the middle of an earthquake. For that 'Rita Tushingham in a black and white movie' look paint a thick black line across the top and bottom lid.

- The 'Cleo' look can be achieved by a thicker and heavier application of a black eyeliner, ending in long point at the end of the eye.
- Buy a proper eyeliner brush, it goes on a lot easier. If you don't want to spend a lot of money then buy a very fine sable-hair artists' brush from a shop that sells that sort of stuff, I don't know how much they are. My eyeliner brush is made from cherrywood and the fine soft quill of a baby hedgehog. It's very good but you do have a problem with fleas.

MASCARA

Can do for you what it did for Theda Bara … A black mascara wand (aptly named) can weave its magic spell and transform stubby pale ginger eyelashes into thick, black, sensuous sweepers. Never use blue mascara – it's common, and brown is boring.

- Black mascara in a little block that you spit on and rub a tiny brush into to coat your lashes is the best, but that's just my personal preference. Amazing mazzys are available on the market, waterproof ones that don't smudge – even if you've been pushed into a canal you'll come up looking gorgeous – your mazzy still intact. Plus you will feel safe in the knowledge that although you are standing in a torrential downpour waiting for a non-existent 41 bus soaked to the skin, your mascara will not have budged – no more Alice Cooper impersonations.
- Apply a coat of mascara across the lower lashes instead of up and down. This way there's less chance of getting it in your face. Apply it coat by coat, building the lash up.
- Remember to coat both sides of your top lashes and get right down to the lid line,

don't just paint the tips. You should never be without mascara – always carry one.

EYE SHADOW

Powdered eye shadow is better than crème which can tend to look greasy and therefore smeared on. What shade you choose is up to you. But if you're going to wear a colour then wear one, pastel shades are too wishy-washy. Why not try 'Aquamarine Flash' a vibrant blue powder from the Flame of Llandudno™ range? Shade the socket with a smoky grey or black, then dust a white shimmering highlighter across the brow bone.

- If using false lashes then use a surgical adhesive to stick 'em on. Don't dye your own eyelashes it will only end in tears – go to a professional.

SPOTS

Has a spot erupted on that clear young teenager skin of yours? Well ha, ha, ha – that's what you get for being young. But don't panic I'm your fairy godmother and I'm going to show you how to zap that zit!

When I was a teenager spots were disguised by a stick of 'Hide the Blemish' concealer. It would transform a humble pimple into a great white mountain with a red dot in the middle, a bit like having a miniature volcano on your face. Tinted medicated concealers in a realistic flesh tone are great if your skin is bright orange, so if you've just been tangoed then this one is for you.

- Dab a spot with a Q-Tip soaked in tea tree oil, a natural antiseptic, then carefully cover the

spot with a tiny amount of green coloured concealer. I'm serious, the green neutralises the red. Blend in, and apply foundation.

- If you still feel that raised bump is in evidence, then turn it into a beauty spot with a black eyebrow pencil. Just dot on or cover in a tiny black velvet patch. Not to be recommended if you have more than two spots or really bad acne. If you are covered in eruptions then instead of moping in your bedroom turn it to your advantage – play bagatelle on your face – simply drop a ballbearing on your forehead and see how long it takes to reach your chin.
- **Never squeeze a spot!**
- Calamine Lotion is great for soothing a red rash. Dab some on before you go to bed. Works well on a shaving rash too fellahs!

INSTANT FACE-LIFTS

- **Beat an egg white and paint a thin coat over your entire face and neck and allow to dry. Watch what happens, it tightens the skin so you can barely speak or blink and then after a while it cracks giving your skin the appearance of an elderly dinosaur's.**
- An elasticated knee support, worn on your head, will give you the most amazing instant face-lift. You need to be wearing a wig or turban to do this. I've never had an occasion to try this, as I never wear a wig, unless it's an acting role and the part calls for it.

- Make up as usual, pop a tubigrip bandage on your head, cover with a wig or turban. There! Twenty years younger, it pulls the skin tight as a drum. Facial expressions are impossible but you'll look fantastic.

FOUNDATION

● 'Peach Princess', a warm natural tint in a panstick form, is perfect for a daytime make-up – use your fingers or a sponge (not the one you clean the car with) for a smooth professional finish. Cover with a dusting of translucent face powder, removing any excess with a brush.

BLUSHER

● Pink or a warm terracotta only, don't go piling on the brick red – you'll only look like a Victorian whore.

TO ACHIEVE CHEEKBONES

● Get your back four teeth removed and smoke low tar fags – sucking these really pulls the cheeks in.
● Have an injection of silicone for the chubby cheek look!

LIPSTICKS

● Either red or pink. Never use a blue or purple lipstick unless you are playing a cardiac arrest victim on Casualty. Brown lipsticks are ridiculous. Who the hell ever had brown lips? It's not natural.
● Draw an outline around your lips before you put your lipstick on to prevent it 'bleeding' and then paint on your lippy – using a brush, it makes it all easier.
● Blood red lipstick makes teeth appear startlingly white. An insipid pink lipstick can make teeth appear yellow.
● Blot with tissue after applying the first coat of lippy, and dust carefully with some face powder to seal it. Reapply another coat

and voila your lipstick will stay put all night – you can even eat a kebab!

● Expensive lip-glosses are a waste of hard earned cash – a tiny amount of Vaseline works wonders. Kathy Kirby used that trick.

● A cheap red lipstick will stain your lips a permanent red – good, isn't that what we want? – so buy cheap lippys. The ones that come free on magazine covers are best, its like gloss paint and won't come off even with a Brillo and Vim.
● When you brush your teeth, brush your lips as well. It gently exfoliates them and will plump them up giving you a fashionable Parisian pout.

EXFOLIATION AND BLEACHING

The epidermis is a layer of dead skin cells so let's slough 'em off and see what's underneath. There is a huge range of exfoliators available on the market but why not save money and have a necking session with a man who needs a shave – the skin will come away in shreds – leaving a layer of new, red raw skin.

● A swollen face can be reduced by popping your head in the freezer for ten minutes, but don't do it in Tesco's 'cos they will only sling you out.
● Hair can be lightened with a chamomile shampoo – it will take about 60 years before it has a noticeable effect so why piss about? Get the 100% peroxide out.

VODKA AND LEMON MASK

Wonderful for toning up the complexion.

- A treble vodka (ice cold), mixed with the juice of a fresh lemon. Pat it on the face, neck and boobs. No need to rinse off, as it will evaporate. You may stink of booze and colleagues will discuss your 'problem' at great length over lunch in the canteen, but what do they know?

WHISKY, YOGHURT AND 'NEW SKIN'

- Whisky can bring a wonderful glow to the cheeks, just drink a bottle and voila – rosy cheeks, eyes and nose.
- Yoghurt is great for sunburn.
- Don't let a cold sore ruin that heavy date. Cover that joey with a coating of 'new skin' and then carefully cover with your concealer and foundation. Apply lippy. He'll never know until he's caught if off you.

CHEMICAL PEELS

- Fruit and hydroxy acids of various strengths are painted onto the skin to peel away those lines. We at The House of Savage™ Skin Rejuvenation Clinic have our own special acid peel, a mixture of caustic soda, Ribena and battery acid that peels the flesh away, revealing that wonderful bone structure.

NATURAL EXFOLIATES

- Take a handful of sugar and mix with olive oil. Rub into your face – pay particular attention to those lines, wipe with a gauze pad and rinse with warm water.

FACE MASKS AND TONERS

- Cat litter makes a wonderful clay mask, providing it hasn't been used by your moggy first. Take a big scoop of it and mix with some water, plaster on your face avoiding the eye area and then rinse with warm water.
- Mayonnaise applied straight from the jar and left on for about 20 minutes is great for dry skin.
- Use a mashed tomato for an oily skin.

- Honey is good for a mature skin, just smear on the gob straight from the hive!
- Mix honey with a ripe banana for an instant face-lift. Mash the ingredients in a cup and smooth on your face, leave it for an hour and then rinse off. You can use it to tighten up any part of your saggy body, if your breasts are hanging like a bloodhound's ears, tighten up with a liberal application and they'll be as firm and hard as the boobs of a young teenager who's been locked in a freezer.
- Slap it on a saggy arse as well!
- There's no need to wash your face of a morning if you cleansed and toned before

MEN
RAZOR BURN

Make your own aftershave balm: mix a spoon of E45 skin cream with a drop of tea tree and lavender oil. This will soothe and calm an irritated skin that's just been shaved.

Only gobshites splash an aftershave on to a freshly shaved face. It don't make you butch because it stings.

you went to bed. **You haven't been working the night shift in a coal mine so leave that soap where it is and just rinse with cold water.**

- A mixture of half rosewater/half witch-hazel makes a refreshing skin toner. Lavender water will soothe a burned or inflamed skin. It will put a fire out as well.
- **Keep toners in the fridge.**

MAKE-UP REMOVER

- **A pure vegetable cooking fat mixed with a few drops of lavender oil make a brilliant make-up remover that will moisturise the skin as well as cleaning it. Pure and economical, but don't go using the fat from the chip pan.**
- Almond oil is a good eye make-up remover, it also nourishes your eyelashes.

BATHROOMS

According to my feminist friends, when you take a bath what you are subconsciously doing is returning to the safety of the womb. Our Vera was greatly influenced by this and she felt the urge to crawl back up into her mother, but since that unfortunate woman's whereabouts are unknown she set about transforming the bathroom instead.

I screamed when I first saw it. Black bin liners covered the entire walls and ceiling, some of them were peeling at the corners where the steam from the bath had softened the blue tack. Lengths of plastic tubes and rubber hose hung suspended from the pulley on the ceiling. Six tennis balls, a football and a cabbage painted luminous green swung next to them, glowing in the ultra-violet light she'd replaced the 100-watt bulb with. I found out later that this was meant to represent the fallopian tubes. I should've realised, shouldn't I? Next to the bath was a great mound of plastic bubblewrap (Vera had nicked an industrial-size reel from China Craft). It glowed from within by the light of a torch and seemed to breathe and pulsate like a giant blob of frog's spawn.

The large extraction pipe from my tumble drier was attached to it with sellotape. It slunk over the bath and the other end was attached to a see-through plastic zip-up suit carrier from Sketchley's the cleaners with my sister, inside, totally naked. She was tapping on the plastic with a bony finger, grinning in the light of a torch she was shining on her face. She looked like the screaming skull or something you might see dangling on a piece of string in a third-rate ghost train. But our Vera was at one with the world. In her amniotic sac attached to the bubblewrap placenta she had gone back to the womb. From the tape machine came the cry of the dolphin, her favourite new age tape, and the air was heavy with the perfume from the cheap scented candles. Unfortunately one of these bloody candles set the bathroom curtains alight – and the house caught fire. Thank God for co-op insurance.

I bought our Vera a flotation tank out of my insurance claim money. She lives in it. Her skin is like a prune. I had to do something about this 'Back to the Womb' craze of hers. She'd wanted a flotation tank ever since she'd heard Ruby Wax had one in her spare room. I'd refused to buy her one so she took to getting in the immersion heater for a few hours as a substitute. Anyway she's blissfully happy now I've given in. It's on trial, mind you, for three weeks with no obligation. I'm hoping the craze passes before then. I'm a martyr, me, a friggin' saint.

BLUE BALLOON CLUB

I made my professional debut at the Blue Balloon Club, my stage name then was Lily La Douce – I thought it sounded French and exotic. The 'Bluey', as it was affectionately known by staff and customers alike, was an intimate cabaret club in Huddersfield, sadly no longer standing, as it was demolished to make way for a supermarket.

I was paid the princely sum of six bob a week, a fortune to me in those days! And boy did we work hard for our money: three shows a night, six days a week, but I loved it. This was showbiz.

The patrons of the 'Bluey' were mostly miners and local factory workers. They were a rowdy lot but very appreciative of my dancing and they would ply me with drinks whenever I sat out front in the bar between shows. This customer relations exercise was encouraged by the management – a charming Greek Cypriot man called Mr Savvas. He was like a father to us girls, always concerned for our welfare. The 'champagne' the customers bought was really just watered down ginger ale.

'I don't want my girls getting bloated with alcohol,' he would say, giving me a friendly pat on the bottom as I squeezed past him in the narrow corridor that led from the dressing room to the stage. It really makes a difference when management shows an interest in their employees' welfare doesn't it?

The girls who worked at the 'Bluey' were a great bunch. The camaraderie in the dressing room that the twelve of us shared was wonderful. I'll never forget the happy times I had there. Now every time I smell Jeyes fluid I'm transported back in time to that cosy little room. I can see it now as if it were yesterday. A dingy cellar with no windows or ventilation, patches of mildew blooming in the damp corners. A make-up shelf ran along the length of one wall, its surface scarred with cigarette burns and sticky with resinous puddles of spirit gum. We sat in front of this applying our stage make-up in the long cracked mirror, its frame surrounded by lightbulbs, some of them actually working.

Our stage costumes hung from a pipe that ran across the room, wall to wall, a worn and motley collection of net bras and G-strings adorned with threadbare tassels and sequinned motifs that might've sparkled fifteen years before when they first made an appearance in 'My Bare Lady', but were now matt and dull from years of sweat and grime, and orange body make-up.

In the corner of the room was a wash basin that was known fondly as the 'Artistes lav'. The acrid smell of stale urine rose from the carpet underneath mixing with other smells in the room: hairspray, Immac hair-removal cream, stale beer, cheap perfume and the heady whiff of greasepaint – showbiz! Marvellous!

I sat next to Gabby Rose Lynn. She was a lovely woman when she was sober but if she was drunk or hungover then there was no talking to her. I think she had a problem. I remember her saying to me one day that her ambition was to be a television presenter, not a stripper. I stared at the tired blonde sitting next to me in her worn kimono applying bleach to her four-inch regrowth and my tender young heart went out to her. What chance did a broken blossom like Gabby have of getting on tv? A woman well past her sell-by date who was

BLUE BALLOON CLUB

LIMEPIT LANE HUDDERSFIELD

PROP. T. SAVVAS

TWELVE! BEAUTIFUL GALS!! TWELVE!
IN OUR BRAND NEW PRODUCTION

TAKE 'EM OFF!

3 SHOWS NIGHTLY

A great little woman

Tiny Tina

Star midget act

The lovely

Gabby Rose Lynn

The Tooting Bec Twirler

Bella The Hun

A 19 stone fantasy in leather

Chrissie Corellie

Huddersfield's dancing daughter

Beauty unadorned

Junie Mae Browne

Princess Zawhore

FULL OF EASTERN MYSTERY

Sandra Hush

'The Ooze'

Sheila

The Slaithwaite stunner

More glamour from

Ruby Arbuckle

CHAMPION WHISTLER AND CLOG DANCER

Gladys AND Pat

Comedy striptease twins

Big and bountiful

BRENDA

Birmingham's answer to Sabrina

First time at the Blue Balloon

Young and dainty Lily LaDouce

a little too fond of the bottle and whose only talent was her ability to swing tassels in time to the music from the end of her pendulous breasts.

'One day, kid,' she said, taking a swig from her can of lager, 'I'll be presenting a Breakfast show, just you wait and see.'

Bella the Hun, a rather large stripper who did an act with a 20 foot python called Freda laughed.

'You?' she scoffed. 'You don't get up 'til tea time, the only time we'll ever see you on telly is when Crimewatch do a profile on you. Breakfast telly indeed!' and she howled with laughter.

'Isn't it time you were milked' sneered Gabby, 'or do those udders of yours always hang so low?'

I miss the witty repartee that was heard in that friendly little room. I did three numbers in the show, the opening number, my solo and the finale.

'Ladeez an' Gentlemen, welcome to the world famous Blue Balloon Club Huddersfield. Are you ready for another evening of gaiety, gags and gals?' came the announcement through the house speakers, the compere's amplified voice roaring through the half-empty club. There was no response from the patrons. 'Suit your fucking selves then,' he said. 'Maybe this will liven you up, best of order around the room for the Blue Balloon Beauties!'

The curtain would part to reveal twelve assorted scantily clad women. Behind us hung a painted backdrop depicting an ornate fountain surrounded by a rose garden in full bloom. Savvas had acquired it from a skip outside the Attercliffe Empire when it was being demolished. Every time the barman opened the fire exit door so he could have a pee in the back alley, the draft would cause the backdrop to bulge forward. The three-piece band struck up a jazzy version of 'In a monastery garden' and we were off!

I did my solo in the second half of the show, a very artistic and tasteful strip that was always well received by the clientele. But the finale was my favourite. We would parade across the stage dressed as Birds of Paradise (I was an emu!) while the band played 'Yellow bird'. It was really quite something to see. Yes, lots of happy memories of the Blue Balloon days!

BEAN BAGS

Just as a single bed pushed against the wall does not a sofa make – a beanbag is a very poor substitute for an armchair. Beanbags should only be used by Alsatians and students. Never attempt to sit on a beanbag if you are very tall and wearing a mini-skirt. Once down you will never get up again without having to crawl on all fours on the floor – very undignified. Take no notice what these home improvement programmes say – there's no need to scatter a few beanbags around if you're furnishing your home on a budget. Get yourself down to Courts – apparently they give sofas away. You don't have to start paying 'til you've had it ten years, and by that time you might have found a better job and be able to afford a couch. Or you can get everything off the catalogue and move.

BORES

I'd sooner be stuck in a lift with a psycho than a bore.

BRITISH JUDICIAL SYSTEM

Derek Bentley,
The Guildford Four
The Birmingham Six
Need I say more?

And what about the Weatherfield One? I'd've put her in the poem but 'one' is a boring word to try and find a rhyme for.

BOY SCOUTS

As a single mother I was always concerned that there was no male influence in our Jason's life. Well, nothing permanent anyway. I was worried that growing up in an all-female household might make it hard for him to relate to men and I felt he needed a male role model. I expressed my concern to Miss Chyat my social worker and for once we agreed.

'I know of a wonderful organisation where he will have the chance to mix and interact with boys of his own age,' she said. Next thing I knew she'd enrolled him in the Boy Scouts.

I remember him coming home after his first 'pack meeting'. I was stood in the back kitchen going through our Bunty's head with a nit comb and a bottle of Suleo.

'Did you enjoy it then love?' I said.
'S'alright,' he grunted.
'What did they teach you then?' I said, removing a big fat mother nit from her clutch of eggs and disposing of her with a loud crack between my nails.

'I learnt how to light a fire and tie a knot,' he replied, not very impressed.

Now I ask you what bloody use is it teaching a kid how to tie a knot and light fires? Alright if you're training them to be pyromaniacs with a fetish for bondage. As it happens 18 months later our Jason was arrested and branded 'The Stockwell Arsonist'. I've always blamed the Scouts, he didn't know what fire was up 'til then, as we'd always had a leccy fire.

'They also taught us how to use a public phone box,' he went on, his voice full of scorn. I couldn't believe it – he'd been breaking into them since he was five. There's nothing our Jason didn't know about payphones. He was very advanced for his age.

'And guess what?' he piped. 'It was a phone-box with your cards in it. I said to Akela, "look at me Mam's business cards!" and he had a good look at them and took them all down.'

I could have died – the cards were innocent enough but the message could have been misinterpreted by a dirty mind. I'd recently learned basket weaving (compulsory in Holloway) so I'd used this talent to earn a few bob at home, a sort of cottage industry. The cards said, 'Chair bottoms recaned. Phone Miss Savage'. Followed by my phone number and there was a little black and white drawing of a woman in boots holding a length of birch. Of course bloody Akela went running to Miss Chyat slandering my good name and this is meat and potatoes to old Chyat. She came round the house the next afternoon.

'I hope,' she said, sitting down uninvited, 'that you are not up to your old tricks again, Lily. We don't want to be doing anything that might be breach of our terms of probation do we?'

I pleaded my innocence, told her I'd gone

into the Repair of Rustic Furniture Business, but she wouldn't believe me. 'Really,' she sniffed. 'Then perhaps we could persuade you to give us a demonstration of the finer points of your craft to the Cubs one evening? I'm sure it would be a learning experience for us all.'

She can be a snotty cow Miss Chyat. She's got a mouth like bee's arse. Well I had no choice did I? Had to go down the Scouts' hut and show the Cubs how to make a lampshade with raffia. They where so impressed that they enrolled me as a den mother. I was given a disgusting uniform to wear and was known as Bagheera. Mind you it was handy. I got the Cubs to put me business cards in phone boxes. They were always going on field trips and hikes – I had cards all over the Wirral, even as far as Southport thanks to the Cubs.

I even went bob-a-jobbing! Although the magistrate called it 'Demanding moneys with menace, prostitution and extortion'. I told him straight. I said that even if I had sunk to the lowest depths of destitution and was starving I wouldn't go giving a wank for a shilling!

Did me no good though. I went off to the Home for Young Ladies and the kids to Rupert and Lucy, the foster parents. Bloody Scouts, don't talk to me about Scouts.

CRABS

Come on, be honest, you've had 'em, haven't you? I have. I caught them off our Vera. There was a time when she had crabs so often she walked sideways. When I say I caught crabs off our Vera, I'm not insinuating that we've had an incestuous relationship, but we have shared a bed on the odd occasion, as sisters do. Vera always used to say, when she discovered yet another infestation, that she'd caught them off a toilet seat. Nothing to do with the fact that she'd had it off with yet another taxi driver! If it wasn't for our Vera, ugly taxi drivers would never get a shag.

Anyway, if you do discover you've got a nest of unwanted lodgers, then here's how to deal with them.

1 For a start, two big tablespoons of honey rubbed into the infected area will rot the little buggers' teeth and prevent them biting. You'll get a good night's kip.

2 Of course if you're full of self-loathing and disgust 'cos you've got pubes that are movin' then this is the only way to shift 'em. It's a bit extreme, but it works and is especially suitable for Born Again Christians and Middle

Englanders who enjoy a bit of flagellation.

- Take a bath in boiling water.
- Shave entire body (including head). Rub a paste made out of caustic soda and bleach into the affected areas with a pan scrub. Scrub vigorously for at least half an hour or until skin bleeds.
- Burn all your clothes, mattress, bedding, pillows, towels, carpets and curtains. Your entire flat should be fumigated (the local council will do this for you – see Yellow Pages for details).
- To ensure you never get these nasty little nippers again, build a sheep dip around your bed. Give all prospective romantic encounters a good dunking.

3 Become a nun/Tibetan monk.

There is one good use for crabs. Pick a couple off and pop 'em in a matchbox with a tiny piece of corned beef so they won't starve. Keep them to flick at people you hate! Pop 'em in your enemy's underwear drawer. I flicked a couple on an *Express* journalist once, but apparently they can only survive on something human.

CAT LITTER

Don't bother with expensive cat litters – use newspapers instead. I try a different paper each day and I've found in my research that the Daily Mail absorbs shit better than any of the others. The Richard Littlejohn column from the Mirror is also very effective. One look at that twisted little nerd's face and my moggies are squatting like good 'uns.

COUNCILS

If you are having trouble getting planning permission for that loft extension or garage, then the golden rule to remember is that all council officials are corrupt lying bastards and it's amazing how quickly things get moving once you've greased their palms with silver. Slip the planning officer a substantial backhander and he'll let you build the Empire State Building in your back yard with no fuss whatsoever.

CREMATION

It's a worry isn't it? What you opt for when the time comes for you to leave this mortal coil. I'm not keen on the idea of being burned so I think I'll probably go for embalming, have my beautifully preserved corpse laid in a glass casket in the middle of a forest with seven dwarfs on permanent vigil. A cousin of my mother's had her husband cremated and she put his ashes in the kid's Etch-a-sketch – a novel and practical way of disposing of them, I thought. Better than sitting in a pot on the mantelpiece doing nothing.

Also there was a woman who lived two streets away from my Mum's house in Birkenhead who shocked everybody at the funeral tea by snorting her husband's ashes from the back of her hand, like snuff, announcing that it was the last hole he was going up. She was a bit common that woman.

Cocktails are real leg-openers. A couple of stingers and a white zombie down me neck and I'm on top of the waiter. A cocktail is guaranteed to make a party go with a zing! Why not try a few at your next social gathering?

COCK

SNOWBALL

The favourite drink of
aunties at Christmas

6 measures of advocaat
2 measures of brandy
drop of lime juice
lemonade

Pour advocaat, brandy and lime juice
into jug and top up with lemonade.
Whisk vigorously.
Transfer to a long glass and serve with a
maraschino cherry and a sprig of mint.
If you run out of advocaat, Windolene
makes an excellent substitute.

DOSSERS' DELIGHT

A cocktail for drinking
outdoors, in parks and
Tube stations.

1 can
Tennent's
Super Lager
Half-bottle
Thunderbird
Half-bottle
Buckfast
1 Bottle
Diamond
White cider
1 Bottle
methylated
spirits
supermarket sherry to taste

Mix in a watering can and then
pass it around! Shout abuse in an
abrasive accent, saying witty things
like 'Gis a ciggy!' or
'Eh?! Arm talkin'
tae yae!'

TAILS

LEG-OPENER

A firm favourite for the gal who is on a tight
budget and wants an immediate result
from her cocktail. One of these will do the
trick.

1 bottle Cherry B
1 pint cider
1 bottle barley wine

Mix and drink very quickly.
After you've come round
you'll find, in fact, your
legs haven't opened
but buckled
underneath
you.

LIME STREET
LULLABY

A cocktail popular
with the streetwalker
of yesteryear, this
cocktail allowed
Maggie May to run
off with the
homeward
bounder's wages.

1 Valium
2 Mogadon
2 Temazepam
4 drops valerian
1 pint lager

Mix ingredients well.
Serve. This drink will
knock him out! (For at least six
hours.)

COMMERCIALS

I think that some of the commercials are better than the programmes. Some of them, though, drive me mad.

'Nicole?'

'Papa?'

'Nicole?!'

'Papa?'

'Nicole get out of the road, a car is coming....'

I've done ads for Ford Motors, Pretty Polly tights and a voice-over for Oasis, a soft drink. Apart from a few voice-overs for regional radio stations as the voice of a budgie and a toilet, that's me lot.

'How could you allow yourself to be the voice of a lavatory,' some piss-elegant journalist asked me once.

Well I'd sooner be the voice of a lav than clean one.

I love doing commercials. I'd do ten a day if I could. You often hear actors saying that they do commercials because it allows them to subsidise other work such as poorly paid rep. My arse! They do 'em because it's ludicrous money for very little work and it's nothing to be ashamed of. It's just a bit of good old honest whoring.

I've always been fond of making a quick and easy buck, but the opportunities to do so are few and far between. You can't get a bloody look in for Vic and Bob, Miss Lumley, Miriam Margolyes and Julie Walters. People ask me do I try the products out before I endorse them. Of course I do. Before I did the budgie advert I ate a packet of Trill just to make sure it was true what the manufacturers claimed – and it is. I bounced down that road, full of health and sunshine vitamins.

I wonder if Joanna Lumley rubs her cheek with the back of a bubble-laden hand every time she washes a dish and says 'Mmm, so soft,' or if Julia McKenzie really licks her lips as she tucks into another lean cuisine? Joanna wouldn't know what a bowl of dirty dishes was let alone what detergent to use and Julia's probably tucking into a nice bit of salmon mousse at the Ivy as we speak.

As it happens, I like the stuff I've done ads for but I'd never advertise a newspaper or promote a product that was tested on animals. Aren't I a goody two-shoes?

My favourites are the Rolo ad, where the elephant remembers that the man in the crowd watching the Circus Parade was the little boy who taunted him years ago, so he slaps him round the gob with his trunk, and the Tango ad. I had endless fun slapping our Vera over the head and shouting 'You've been tangoed' as I sprayed her with a can of orange paint. Yes, I like the commercials and I'm open to offers so 'Open, pour, be a whore once more!'

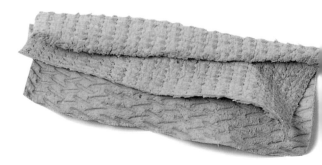

CLEANING

I hate cleaning. Who doesn't? Life's too short to clean an oven and as far as I'm concerned a hoover is something you hang your coat on when you return from a night's revelry. I got the hoover out two years ago and it's sat in the same place in the hall ever since. They scare me, hoovers.

I used to be a char when I was a struggling

actress. For a while I worked for an agency called Scrubbers. I had gone in to sign up as I originally thought the agency was involved in a different line of work. I had no idea it was a cleaning agency. Anyway, I was skint, so needs must.

How I hated cleaning other women's houses. For a pound an hour I'd scrub and polish. I'd wash their fancy dishes, me own tears falling into the soap suds. I haven't washed a dish since. I've got a dishwasher now and it was the best money I've ever spent. It changed my life that dishwasher, no more rubber gloves for me, unless I've got a punter with certain tastes that is.

Even though I hate housework I haven't got a cleaner – no thanks. I'd sooner live with the dust knee-deep than have a chirpy lady 'who does' throwing the hoover around. Also they might find something indiscreet and go to the press. You've got to be careful when you're a sex kitten in the public eye.

When I was a cleaning lady I used to read every diary and letter I could get my hands on and since I cleaned the homes of the rich and famous I gleaned some very interesting information. The objects I found under the beds, I could tell tales. I won't though as long as they continue to keep sending me hush money each week. My lips are sealed.

If you are a cleaner then here's a few good tips to make your chores seem lighter.

- **If your employer is out, squirt lots of Pledge and air freshener in every room. It will smell like you've really given it a good going over. Do the same to the mouthpiece of the phone and when your employer uses it they will smell it and think how lucky they are to have such a thorough and diligent domestic.**

- Hoover and polish a few bits and pieces, and then collapse on the sofa to watch a bit of tv.

- **Help yourself to a bottle of their wine – they can afford it and they won't miss it.**

- Have your pals in to show them round, try on 'madam's' clothes, laugh at their family photos and learn about their most intimate secrets by reading their diaries and letters.

- **Blackmail 'em. Cleaning for other people can be an interesting and lucrative career if you know the right way to go about it.**

CELEBRITY

Being in the public eye means you can no longer run down to the Netto with no slap on and last night's dinner down your cardie, because you can guarantee that a member of the paparazzi will snap a sly photo and you'll end up in the Sunday Mirror Magazine with a 'witty' caption.

A lot of celebs moan about having no privacy, or being unable to walk down the street or shop at Tesco because the adoring public keep mobbing them. If I feel the need for privacy I resort to disguise. A black headscarf, a black mac and dark glasses à la Jackie O guarantee my anonymity. I've even been known to dress as a man. You'd never guess it was me. I look like a very smart lesbian.

Oh! No!

FIRST FOR ALL THE NEWS

ISSUE 127 • SEPTEMBER 18 1998 • £1.45 WEEKLY

THE TRUTH
ABOUT LILY
AND ROBBIE

Oh! No! EXPOSES
THE FACTS ABOUT
LILY SAVAGE'S
SECRET AFFAIR WITH
ROBBIE WILLIAMS

INSIDE:
TINA HOBLEY'S
BATHROOM

TINA HOBLEY'S
BACK BEDROOM

D

DRUGS

My first experience with drugs was in Amsterdam. I had taken advantage of an offer for cheap weekend breaks on the back of a packet of Omo soap powder, and I was taking a stroll with our Vera looking for a cafe to have a bit of dinner. Our Vera was going through her vegan stage and refused to eat anywhere that sold meat. Anyway we came upon a caf with a leaf stuck in the window, the international symbol for vegetarian food, or so we thought – we didn't realise that the leaf was from the cannabis plant until we were well into our third slice of 'space cake'. Talk about stoned. The rest of that weekend is a blur, not an unpleasant one, but a blur all the same. Dope makes you hungry. Its called 'the munchies'. I was so hungry I could've eaten a nun's arse through the Convent railings. I came back from Amsterdam two stone heavier.

My daughter Bunty went on a camping trip to Epping Forest with the probation service and bought a bag of magic mushrooms back with her. She left them on the kitchen table and, thinking they were your common as garden field mushroom, I fried them with a nice bit of back bacon for my breakfast. Three weeks later I was found in the back of a dress shop swigging Brasso and singing 'Stormy Weather'. I could've killed our Bunty, but she said it was my own fault for not realising that the mushrooms were 'magic'. Apparently you can tell the difference because magic mushrooms have a chimney on the roof and a little man with a red cap and beard mending boots – silly me!

Somebody gave me an 'E' once. I put it in the back pocket of my slacks and forgot about it until I came to wash them. I popped my slacks, 'E' and all, into the washing machine and do you know that it was on the spin cycle for eight hours. It drank about 50 gallons of water. Every time I turned Radio 1 on the Zanussi would start raving.

I do think they should decriminalise cannabis and make it legal. I'm also for controlling 'E'. You go in a disco these days and nobody's drinking booze anymore, everyone's on 'E' and it makes people 'touchy, feely and very friendly'. You don't get like that after a bottle of Scotch – quite the opposite for some people – yet you can buy it quite openly. So until this government stops burying their heads in the sand and refusing to do something to control 'E', young people will still continue to buy it from shady dealers outside rave venues or night clubs, not knowing what the fuck is in it. Everything from embalming fluid to rat poison is used to make cheap 'E'. A controlled drug would at least be safe. Hasn't anyone learned anything from the folly of prohibition when the sale of alcohol was outlawed and home-made bootleg gin, produced in bathtubs, was readily available in speakeasies? A gin that would rot your guts and make you blind? It's the same situation with 'E'. The government should also make Drugs Education compulsory in all schools. Prevention is better than cure – get them while they are young. I despair sometimes. I might run for parliament. They could do with a bit of glamour in the 'house'.

DISNEY

remember my Mam taking me to see Walt Disney's Sleeping Beauty cartoon. I was terrified. I screamed the place down and had to be taken out. She'd thought that Sleeping Beauty would be an ideal birthday treat (I'd just turned 32) and I was really enjoying the film until that bloody princess Aurora appeared and sang 'Once Upon A Dream' with an owl and a couple of squirrels. All that panting! All that cooing! That peasant frock! The hair! AAAAAAGH! Mother! Get me out of here!

DENMARK

Copenhagen, cold and depressing but very pretty and spotlessly clean. The only rubbish you see on the streets of Copenhagen are the Fins, Swedes and Norwegians who collapse where they stand after a night on the piss. Well, they can't get booze in their own country so they have to go to Denmark if they fancy a bevvy. Drunken bodies lying all over the pavements and roads – thank God we never see that kind of thing in Birkenhead.

DIARIES

'Always keep a diary and some day it will keep you.'
So said that wise old bird Mae West.

I've never managed to keep a diary – I start out with good intentions on the first day of every new year and diligently record every last detail of the day's exciting events but by the time I get to the third of January I've lost interest, so the rest of the year goes unrecorded. I wish I had've kept it up but I can't be arsed and beside what do I want to see my most personal secrets down in print for? I can pick up a newspaper if I want to read things like that.

Our Vera has always kept a diary ever since she was a nipper. She's not speaking to me at the moment (yawn) – we had a big row last night. She claims that I interfere in her life! She says that I'm intrusive nosy and constantly invade her privacy, well to be honest she didn't exactly tell me this herself . . . I read it in her diary. Serves her right for leaving it hanging about in a locked box under the floorboards. I couldn't resist having a little peek and I am glad I did. To prove to you what kind of do-lally psycho bitch I have to put up with I've torn a week out her diary and reprinted it here, without the authoress's permission (I can't ask her if she's not speaking to me, now can I?)

I'm a martyr me, a bloody martyr.

JULY 1998

MONDAY Woke up at ½ 3 this morning crippled with indigestion so I had to get up and take 2 Rennies and a Gaviscon. Woke up again at 7 because I was bursting for a wee. Took a painkiller in case I get one. Went back to bed but have to get up at 8 because I've got to go for a Restart. Had a boiled egg for me breakfast. FED CATS. The bloke in the restart asked me what sort of job I thought that I could train for so I said I wouldn't mind being a stewardess or a Vet. He asked what I'd been doing with myself during me period of unemployment.

'Miss Cheeseman' he said. 'What have you been doing with your life?'

So I said I was writing a book about our Lily's life but I asked him not to say owt as our Lily doesn't know about it yet.

Then he asked me if I thought my writing could support me so I said look at that Andrew Morton and Kitty Kelley, they made a fortune and they didn't even have any juicy photos to back there stories up, but I have and I showed him the picture of our Lily on the bathroom floor after Elton's party.

He asked me if anyone had shown me any interest or made an advance so I said not since I went to see Terms of Endearment at the Plaza and a dirty old man put his hand on my leg.

Anyhow I start work next Monday as a cleaner in an old people's home I'm not fucking going. Bought 2 Scratchcards, lost went home. Had me tea watched Corry, washed out a vest and some draws went to bed early because I think I'm getting a cold.

TUESDAY

Woke up at ½ 3 again with a splitting headache. Had a mug of Daynurse and a Beechams and went back but I couldn't get off. She came in at ½ 6 blind drunk, she's been out all night and she brought two fellahs back with her. She was shouting Vera get up I've got you a fellah outside me door. So I got up and took me rollers out had a wash and put me black nightie on but when I went into the front room he'd gone home so I got dressed and went to the doctor.

Gave me my prescription and he's arranging for me to go in an iron lung. I can't wait. Went down to me mate's but she wasn't in. The woman next door said she was up the hospital having her electrics shock therapy. She normally goes on a Wednesday but they've changed the day apparently.

Went home she was up. I said who was that Fellah. And she said what Fellah. There was no Fellah in this house you must be seeing things Vera. She looks terrible ha ha serves her right made the tea, she's still got a hangover and can't face food or she'll throw up. Made boil in the bag parsley sauce mashed spuds peas and a sweetbread. Our Lily vomited all over the hall carpet. Ha Ha. Jason came in about ½ 9 with a Balti for us all our Lily was lying on the couch and caught a whiff of it and spewed up her ring again. She had to go to bed Ha Ha. I eat her Balti and half of Jason's watched a film on the video and went to bed.

WEDNESDAY

Woke up at 2 in the morning with shocking diarohea sat on the lav till 6. It must be the Balti. Waited till 8 and went to the Doctor's because this is so bad it must be a colli. Got a bottle of medicine and I can't eat for 24 hours, nothing, he said just liquids. Went to the pub on the way home and had two pints of Guinness and a Vodka and tonic. Came home about half eleven. She was smashing the house up because she didn't get nominated for a BAFTA. She said how was she supposed to make quality telly when she was surrounded by twats and then she started on me saying I was drunk. I wasn't drunk I'd only had a couple and she's got a cheek to call anyone a drunk. Went to me room and when I heard her going out I got up and watched the video. I'd videoed Pet Rescue and there are two lovely donkeys that are looking for a good home so I'm going to ring up in the morning and get them. It must be 24 hrs by now so I'm going to make myself a boiled ham barm cake and eat the other sweetbread I'm starving.

THUSDAY

Rang the women on Pet Rescue and said I was Miss Savage's personal secretary and that she had been moved by the plight of the donkeys and was offering them a comfortable home. She said that they normally insist on a home check but because 'the thing' is so well known they didn't have to bother. They are delivering the donkeys on Saturday. Rang up the Sun and told Gary that our Lily was adopting donkeys he said it was typical of our Lily she's got a huge heart. I think he said heart this bloody portable keeps breaking up. Anyway there coming on saturday as well and she won't dare throw the donkeys out in front of them. She'll have to let me keep them.

FRIDAY Woke up at ½7 in agony. My head was banging and me guts are still bad. I've got E Colli. Got up she's still not in yet the dirty cow. Got dressed went for a paper and me ciggies. She's all over the front of the Daily Mirror blind drunk with her tongue down Robbie Williams' throat. Dirty Bitch if she touches Robbie I'll kill her. She's old enough to be his Granny and she looks it in the photos she looks about 60, no 90 no she looks TWO HUNDRED. I love Robbie and she's only doing it to spite me the fucking sly cow.

I HATE HER

She came home about 6pm and went mental. I was trying to soften me corn so I could use me new corn cutter which looks fabulous and she started banging on the kitchen window wanting to know why I was sat on the draining board with me foot in the sink, sat in the window like an Amsterdam tart, she's the tart not me. She got changed and went out again. I said will you be coming home tonight. And she said she was only going to supper with a friend. Supper! Who does she think

SATURDAY she is. She's no stranger to an outside lav. Put me rollers in went to bed she came home about 3. I think she's drunk good.

Gary Bushell and a Sun photographer arrived at about ½ 10 she's just got up and was sat in the kitchen in her housecoat & rollers with no make-up on looking like shit. She nearly died when I brought them into the kitchen and shot upstairs to get dressed. I made them a cup of tea and told them to have a good look around, help themselves. I put a packet of King Size Rizzla on the mantlepiece where they could see them. She came down painted up to the nines all airs and graces, she's such a fucking creep she makes me sick.

Gary said 'Where's the donkeys' and she said 'I haven't done that act since I worked in Cairo, you know that Gary. And laughed a phoney laugh like the big phoney she is. He asked her about Robbie and she said there was nothing she could say just yet and patted her belly, who does she think she's kidding she hit the menopause years ago. Then the donkeys arrived, you could see she wanted to go berserk but she just smiled for the photographers. There on the balcony now, lovely things I'm calling them Matt and Luke after Bros. She's gone to bed with a valium, she says she can't take any more, good. Had a wash, fed donkeys + cats and the others went to bed

SUNDAY

One of the Donkeys kicked the balcony door open in the middle of the night and wandered into her bedroom one of them got on the bed and went to sleep. She didn't wake up as she was full of pills. When she did she screamed the house down. I sat on the bed and laughed me head off!!

I ran out of me room pretending to be concerned and slipped in a big pile of donkey business in the hall. I was covered in it, even in my rollers. She laughed her head off, thought it was funny— Cow.

She rang a donkey sanctuary in Southport up to see if they would take them they said they would if she gave 'em ten grand. She had to say it and we all know how she hates to part with money so she's got the roaring hump. I'm glad Cilla rang wanting her hover mower back. I cut me corn while she was out getting her nails done. Wrote a chapter of the book about her and Emperor Roscoe in Amsterdam. Corn bleeding had me tea watched telly went to bed.

MONDAY

Woke up early. Me foot is like the elephant man's it's twice the size of a normal foot. It must be infected with gangrene. Rang an ambulance. Got taken to the General in the ambulance. I've only got one shoe on. Had to wait ages to be seen I was left sitting there me foot getting bigger and bigger but they don't care these nurses you could die under their nose and they wouldn't know. Saw the doctor eventually after waiting a full half hour he said my corn was septic and the foot had become infected and asked me if I'd been cutting it so I said no. I got some antibiotics and a sick note so I don't have to report for my duties at the old peoples home! Brilliant!

Bunty came to pick me up in the car our Lily stayed at home because she thinks if a big star like her went into a hospital waiting room she'd be mobbed by adoring fans.

Kylie Marie is four on Tuesday I must rob her a present. Went home, got no sympathy off her she's got the hump because she found my hedgehog in the airing cupboard. The Southport donkey sanctuary came to collect Matt and Luke. Thank fuck for that said Lily after they'd gone. I had a little cry in my bedroom then sniffed some poppers so I felt better. Watched Songs of Praise. It was from Norwich this week, it was good drank 3 bottles of wine with our Lily and Bunty and played cards till ½ 12. Had me foot up on the pouffe and Lily kicked it. The pain I'm sure she did it deliberately, went to bed.

DOGS

Buster Elvis Savage – alias 'The Todge' – is my dog and I love him. He might try to shag my leg and let off in bed, but then I've known fellahs like that. I'd sooner have my Buster in the bed than a husband. He doesn't lie to me, nick my purse or watch sport all day on the telly. Neither does he come home drunk (well, only occasionally), pee in the kitchen sink or stub his tab end in my bowl of pot pourri. Okay, he might run me phone bill up dialling 0898 numbers, but then no one's perfect.

Buster and me first met three years ago when he was brought into the Big Breakfast studios, a tiny abandoned puppy. He tottered across the studio floor and sat on my foot. It was love at first sight.

He goes everywhere with me. He's been in a helicopter with a pair of Walkman headphones on and he treats the BBC like he owns it. And why shouldn't he? My Buster gets more fan mail than that mongrel on Blue Peter and he's constantly inundated with requests to do dog food commercials. I always turn them down on his behalf – I don't approve of exploiting animals and, besides, they didn't offer enough wonga.

Everybody wants to know what breed Buster is. His pedigree is a great mystery; in fact it's been the subject of discussion on Question Time. Well, let me tell you: Buster is a shit-tzu – with something in him. Some folk say he's a Lhasa apso or bichon frise. Andrew Duncan who writes for the Radio Times said he was a poodle, but then what would that old fool know? You never say the 'P' word in front of Buster. He reacts very badly.

As far as he's concerned his mother was a shit-tzu and his father was a pit bull, and that's what he tells the press.

Buster is a true showbiz dog. 'He was born in a handbag,' a major tv star at eight weeks old, in the West End at ten weeks, and two national tours and a summer season under his belt by the time he was one. Nothing fazes him, he's a fearless little individual who knows his own mind. His favourite person is Quentin, the BBC floor manager, and his hobbies are hanging out of moving car windows and sitting in the front window and barking if a burglar appears. His favourite food is chicken. In fact he'd eat anything except dog food and he loves ice cream. He loves children and he never bites. He's wonderful in hotel bars. He'll weave in and out of the chairs, nicking purses from women's handbags and putting the loot under my chair. I'm innocent in all this – I've had some very embarrassing moments in hotels trying to explain why I have six stolen purses around my feet.

If you want to join Buster's fan club, 'The Buster Club', please send a cheque or postal order for 300 quid payable to L. Savage, and we will send you a comprehensive catalogue of Buster merchandise. How about a genuine silver-plated dog bowl that plays 'Edelweiss' when your dog eats from it?

DIVORCE

When my divorce finally came through I stood outside Birkenhead Town Hall after the hearing and sobbed. I can't say exactly how I felt, as I was a mass of mixed emotion. I was relieved that I had severed all ties with the bastard but there was an underlying shame. I felt I'd failed. My marriage, albeit brief, had collapsed and I was single again. Damaged goods – a shop-soiled dee . . . vor . . . cee.

My Mam and our Vera came with me to the court. Me mother was a tower of strength – she'd dragged me off to the pub for a badly needed drink to help repair my tattered nerves. Our Vera tactful as ever put 'D.I.V.O.R.C.E.' on the jukebox and as Tammy's beautiful voice filled the air I dissolved into tears once again.

'I've let the family down' I sobbed. 'I've brought shame on the name of Savage. Oh Mam I'm the first person in our family to ever get divorced.'

Me mother took a swig of her drink and belched. 'That's because you're the only one to ever get married – now stop your whinging and get them in.' She was a wonderful woman my mother – so wise.

My daughter Bunty's marriage ended in divorce as well. I said her marriage wouldn't last, she should never've married in the first place. I told her she'd rue the day, but she wouldn't listen. I was exactly the same at her age – I suppose what's in the bitch comes out in the pup.

Our Vera's first marriage was annulled by the Pope because it was never consummated. Our Vera was still virgo intacto after the wedding night. (See V for Vera). She married again but that was even worse. It's all very sad – we refer to it all as 'the great tragedy'.

I do believe, though, that if a marriage isn't working and life is unbearable then it's time to cut your losses and bail out. Sometimes marriage isn't a word, it's a sentence. I knew that the sun had set on my marriage when my ex-husband asked me what I'd like for Christmas and all I could think of was a widow's pension. I can remember my wedding like it was yesterday. I wish it was tomorrow because I wouldn't go.

I stood at the altar on my wedding day not with my husband-to-be at my side, but a screw from Walton. He was handcuffed to Bill who had permission to leave the nick for an hour to get married. The priest didn't know who was the groom and I nearly became the wife of a Prison Officer until I pointed out his mistake to him. I should've kept my mouth shut. As much as I dislike jailers at least he had a steady job, which is more than can be said for Billy Boy and I might be still be happily married to this day.

But there's no point crying over spilt milk, I was never cut out to be a wife so let's leave it at that. My advice to any woman considering marriage would be to live with him for couple of years before taking the plunge. You want to know what you're getting, and will you still feel the same way about him when he lets off in bed and holds your head under the Duvet cover?

DRIVING

I'd always cracked on that I was never interested in learning to drive. Cars bored the arse off me. 'As long as it gets me from A to B,' I would say, 'I don't mind what make it is.' Well, guess what? I was lying.

Oh, how I dreamt of driving along a country lane at the wheel of an open-top sports car. The radio on full belt, a headscarf to protect the barnet from the wind, dark glasses, a camel car coat and a pair of those driving gloves with holes in the back of the hand. A sophisticated, independent woman of the 90s who can go

any place, anywhere, anytime. Like a Martini. I'd see little old women driving cars and I'd think, if they can do it then surely to god so can I.

But it was the night I saw Dale Winton's car that finally made me send off for a licence and learn to drive.

An old flame rang me up out of the blue and asked if I'd like to go away with him for the weekend. Of course I said 'yes'. He arranged to pick me up after work (I was recording Blankety Blank at the BBC) but I had to meet him outside the studio gates away from prying eyes. We had to be discreet as he was a very prominent public figure and also I have my reputation to think of. (The publishers aren't paying me enough to reveal my old flame's identity. This is not a kiss and tell book, so he shall be known as Mr X unless they bung me another few quid.)

Anyway, after I'd recorded the show, I got changed into a black cocktail frock, collected my cases from my dressing room and rushed off for my assignation. I bumped into Dale Winton in the corridor.

'Where are you going Lil?' he asked, 'anywhere you shouldn't be?'

I told him where I was off

to. He's got that kind of open face, Dale, that makes you feel you can confide in him. Of course he was thrilled to bits and rushed off to tell Barbara Windsor.

Standing on the pavement outside the Beeb with me suitcases and the dog, I was approached by a 'gentleman of the road'. 'Have you bin thrown out of your lodgings then?' he asked, looking at my luggage.

'It's no fun is it love, living rough, especially at our age?' He took a swig from the can he was holding and shook his head. 'One bad winter and you'll be pushing up daisies.'

I stared at this old bugger. He must have been at least 75 and obviously a bit 'confused' to mistake me for a woman of his age group. After bumming a fag off me he introduced himself as 'Tommo' and told me that there was a hostel in King's Cross that would probably take me in for the night but they wouldn't allow pets.

'Your best bet, Ma' he said, 'is to get rid of the dog. Sell it.'

'Sell my dog?' I shrieked. 'Sell Buster? I'd sooner sell my body first!'

'Aye,' he said, giving me the once over, 'but you'll get more for the dog.'

I ignored this remark. This man was a deranged drunk who didn't know what he was on about. I picked Buster up and held him against my protective bosom, whispering in his ear, 'Whoose de bessie liddle boyden fer his mam den ay, whoo is?' The shit we come out with when we're making a fuss of a baby or a cute dog.

(When our Kylie-Marie was a podgy little baby I used to blow a raspberry on her bare little belly or suck her little toes and fingers and say: 'Ooh! I could eat you.'

When you think about it, 'I could eat you' is a strange thing to say to a 6-month-old baby. In the dark recesses of our minds is some primitive instinct still lurking, that makes us crave human flesh? Succulent milk-fed meat to satisfy our primeval desires? I read somewhere that our prehistoric ancestors liked to indulge in a bit of cannibalism.)

I was cursing Mr X for leaving me standing in the street at the mercy of drunks, when suddenly the most beautiful car I've ever seen drove out of the main gates. The tinted glass window opened with an electronic purr and from inside this pulling machine I could hear the voice of Sheila Tracey on the radio announcing the 'BBC Big Band' conducted by Barry Forgie with a medley from Oklahoma!

The driver of this elegant car leaned out of the open window. It was Dale Bloody Winton.

'Oh, hello, you still here?' he said, staring incredulously at Tommo. 'Is this your fellah?' he mouthed quietly to me, 'Fancy!'

'Give us a lift son,' said Tommo, peeing up the side of a lamppost, forcing me to act quick and move me suitcase, before the fast flowing river of Tennent's Extra running down the pavement soaked it. 'We need to get to King's Cross to get a bed for the night.'

'Taking you to a hotel is he?' said Dale, still in his Les Dawson voice. 'A bit of rough trade for the weekend, what are you like?' Before I could explain Dale drove away.

'Love to give you a lift but I'm going the other way, sorry. Byeee.'

I stared with a mixture of envy and lust as this gorgeous, gleaming beauty of a car drove away. My eyes were glazed. Like Mr Toad I was hooked.

'It's that fuckin' dog's fault,' said Tommo, staggering around the pavement, trying to button his fly. 'You never get a lift with a dog. People don't want a smelly dog in their car, pissing all over the place.'

I said nothing. Grabbing my bare arm with a wet hand Tommo pulled me towards him.

'I have to tell you,' he said, 'I travel alone. You'll have to go your own way. Stop bothering me.' And then as an after thought he added 'No offence, Ma.'

I flagged a passing cab and went home to make a wax effigy of Mr X, but instead of sitting in the back of the cab, my cheeks burning with indignation and humiliation at having been stood up, all I could think of was Dale's tasty motor.

The next week I went on a crash driving course. By that I don't mean crashing the car, I mean you learn in a week and then take your test at the end of it. Before I could even get in the car I had to do a written test.

How boring is the Highway Code? I forced myself to learn it. Some of the road signs are pointless if you ask me. The one that has a drawing of a leaping stag on it. How many stags have you come across leaping on the road? Or falling rocks? I shit myself when I come to a falling rock sign – I thought I was about to encounter an avalanche.

I went to great lengths to learn the friggin' Highway friggin' Code. I went to bed each night and would fall asleep listening to a tape explaining the different road signs. While I was unconscious someone swapped tapes, probably Vera, my simple-minded slut of a sister, and replaced the 'Highway Code' with 'Learn a Foreign Language in a Week' which explains why I sometimes come out with a bit of Polish when I've had a bevvy.

I took ten lessons in an automatic. I tried in a car with gears first, but I couldn't be arsed with it – pullin' and pushin'. With an automatic you just switch on and go – it's like driving an armchair.

Our Jason was against me driving. He gave

me a couple of lessons in one of his cars (he's been driving since he was 6) and had the cheek to say I'd never make a driver. I had a couple of lessons off a bloke who used to drive get-away cars and his complaint was that I drove too fast – you think he'd be used to racing down the high street at 80 mph, considering his profession, bloody wimp.

Well the great day came – my test date. I set off to the test centre with a statue of St. Jude, a lucky Joan the Wad, a lump of coal, a horseshoe and some heather in my handbag – just for luck. To make sure I was alert I'd been taking Ginko Biloba by the shovelfull and laying off the temazepam. I even got the Aunties' spell book out and found a powerful potion that when drunk allowed you to pass any exam. I'd left the newly brewed potion in the kitchen to cool and our Vera, thinking that it was alcoholic, drank it. She's really pissed off now because she passed her Social Security Medical and they took her off the sick and told her to look for work – a four letter word that has the same effect on Vera as garlic does on a vampire.

Anyway, my driving test examiner was a woman and as she wasn't a lez, the short skirt was a waste of time.

At the end of the test she told me to pull over. I was feeling pretty pleased with myself but the examiner soon blew the wind out of my sails. She had a face like a smacked arse and sat in her seat, shaking, staring straight ahead.

'What happened back there then at the zebra crossing?' she asked.

'Don't start fucking nit picking now,' I thought. 'You're lucky we got this far, alive and in one piece.'

I didn't say this, I smiled instead and asked casually, 'It was only a little mishap, nothing to worry about surely?'

'You hit somebody,' she said, her voice shaking. 'And you refused to stop the vehicle.'

The 'somebody' I'd hit was our Vera. She was making her way home from the Off Licence, a bit pissed, and she just wandered into the road. I could've swerved, but I thought bugger it, and put me foot down. I don't know what came over me. She was flung 22 ft. into the air, her brolly opened and she landed safely in the playground of the local junior school. The kids thought it was Mary Poppins.

'And what do we do when we see a red light?' said the examiner, nearly hysterical by now. She's stuck her pen in her hair and was twisting it round and round. If you want my opinion she was far too highly strung to be a driving examiner.

'Well,' I said, 'it depends where the red light is. If it is in the front parlour window of a single woman's house then I would assume that she was an enterprising woman, earning some extra cash by working at home. If it's on the end of a pole by the side of the road, I'm almost sure that it means stop.'

'Then why the fuck didn't you?' she screamed, losing the plot completely and bashing me over the head with her clipboard. I complained about her afterwards but it was no good – I failed.

That night I sat on the couch in the dark, a suicidal wreck. Me, Mrs Savage's little girl, a failure. I sat in the dark and thought about all the things I couldn't do as a non-driver: make full use of the car service in Marks & Spencer's or go to a drive–in McDonalds, and I'd never be able to visit a Safari Park. Life can deal some cruel blows can't it?

I'm not giving up though. I'm having more lessons and another test date has been set. I'll let you know ...

EARLY MORNINGS

I'm not what you would describe as a morning person. To be blunt I feel like shit and I look like shit. I've never been one of these early risers who leap out of bed and throw the curtains open to greet the dawn with a cheery smile. I haven't opened my bedroom curtains since I put them up ten years ago and that's how its staying. A bedroom should be like a tomb – PITCH DARK.

I've always woken up like the wrath of God. I've had more arguments and fights with people of morning – my tolerance level is nil and the temper thermometer has risen to rattlesnake-with-toothache level. I wish people would leave me alone when I get up. I'll admit I'm foul tempered and unreasonable in the crucial early hours, but I'm O.K. after a while. So piss off and leave me to thaw out and I won't attack you with a chainsaw.

I need silence of a morning. No telly or radio and no people with irritating habits – hoovering is a hanging offence and a persistently ringing telephone will find itself ripped from the wall and flung out of the window and into the back garden, which is beginning to resemble a telecom graveyard.

I need to sit, in stunned silence, with a pot of tea and ten fags staring into space for at least an hour before I can be classified 'human'.

I'm definitely not in my right mind first thing, I could KILL, and I often wonder if our Vera is aware that as she mooches about the kitchen making her breakfast, rattling cutlery and crashing dishes in the sink, a schizo psychopath with a PhD in mental cruelty is silently observing her.

I went to the doctor to see if she could give me something that might improve my mood.

'An early night perhaps?' she suggested sweetly. She did a test to see if it was PMT. I went back for the results a week later.

'We've had the results back,' she said, 'and it's not PMT.'

'What is it then?' I asked.

'Nothing. You are just a bad-tempered bitch.'

I've changed doctors since. Sex of a morning is out of the question – I don't care how much they're paying. Nothing and I mean nothing OR no-one would enduce me to have a bit of bloomer

work in the morning. They might as well shag a corpse.

So be afraid, be very afraid and take heed of this warning – keep away from me of a morning and you might live to tell the tale.

ELVIS

The King, gone but not forgotten by me and his millions of fans all over the world. I love Elvis – I could listen to 'Love Me Tender' all day. There'll never be another star like Elvis. I've made a little shrine to the great man in the corner of my bedroom. It's very simple, just a card table covered with my Elvis headscarf, a couple of candles and a framed photo of him from the film Viva Las Vegas. I kiss it every night before I go to bed, you can hardly see his face for pink lipstick smudges.

Actually, the photo has got Ann Margret in it as well. I couldn't cut her out because he's got his arm around her and that would've meant a one-armed Elvis, so I cut my face out of a photo and stuck it over hers. It's very realistic, you'd actually think it was me with the King. No such luck I'm afraid.

I've also got an Elvis wall hanging that used to hang in the boudoir when I was on The Big Breakfast. I brought it home with me when I left because I knew that when Vanessa Feltz took over she'd want to redecorate my beautiful salon to suit her own taste. Elvis and gold flock wallpaper don't exactly go well together, so he's now hanging on my bedroom wall, surrounded by leopardprint wallpaper at three quid a roll in majestic splendour.

Even my radio alarm clock has got Elvis on it. A twelve-inch model of the King dressed in his famous silver lamé-suit mounted on an onyx base. When the clock goes off, instead of an annoying electronic beep waking me from my slumber I'm gently eased into the day with 'You Ain't Nothin' but a Hound Dog'. The model gyrates back and forth in time to the

music. It's very realistic and all my pals love it.

I have to say, albeit regrettably, that I don't believe that the King is still alive. According to the Sunday Sport comic he is alive and well and working in a Burger King in Toledo. What rubbish, and what an insult to the memory of the King of Rock and Roll.

Callous as it may sound, dear reader, it's probably better to die young when you're a legend. You get to keep your dignity. Otherwise as you get older you may find yourself on a game show or in Dallas. Marilyn would probably be in Falcon Crest, James Dean would be advertising adult incontinence pads on US telly and Dame Thora wouldn't be the one scorching up the stairs in a Stannah chair lift – it would probably be Elvis.

ELVIS PRESLEY, THE KING.

REST IN PEACE.

ETIQUETTE

IN TODAY'S SELFISH AND UNMANNERED SOCIETY, where gentlemen are few and far between, and ladies drink pints and pull their knickers out from between the cheeks of their arse in public, a well-mannered, cultured person is as rare as our Vera in full-time employment. Common civility costs nothing and I firmly believe that children should be taught a conventional code of conduct. My kids have beautiful manners. Our Jason may be a car thief but he always leaves a thank you note on the pavement. If you have impeccable manners you can move in any society with confidence and grace. You may have a face like a robber's dog and live in a caravan but it doesn't matter as long as you know how to eat asparagus in the proper manner. Your physical shortcomings and humble lifestyle will be forgiven.

So, my ill-bred, uncouth friend, allow me to elucidate the finer points of etiquette.

One of my dearest pals is Lady Joyce Parsons. If you read Tatler and The Field then you will be familiar with this famous London socialite. I'm frequently invited to spend the weekend at her country seat, Parson Hall, a fine old stately home in Berkshire. I wasn't born with a silver spoon in me mouth – to be honest, it was a tin-opener – but I know how to conduct myself and I'm certainly not intimidated by that kind of environment. And neither will you be after you've read my guidelines on how to behave in society.

THE COUNTRY HOUSE WEEKEND

*W*hat do you do if you're invited to the country for the weekend by one of the nobs? Panic? No you don't! You might be a bit of a scrubber but remember the old saying: 'The colonel's lady and Judy O'Grady are sisters under the skin!' A handle in front of their name doesn't make them any better than you. Some of the aristocracy have appalling manners. Ever seen a debs' ball? Right pack of snotty scrubbers in tulle frocks trying to get their leg over with a bunch of chinless, pissed-up Hooray Henrys. And watching Princess Margaret eating her dinner isn't a pretty sight. She never looks up – just shovels everything put before her down her gob and grunts.

So calm down, take a sheet of your best, heavily scented notepaper and write a reply accepting your hostess's kind invite – immediately, in case they change their mind. A hostess can get very pissed off if you just turn up unannounced. I won't open my front door unless I'm expecting someone – you don't know who it is, do you? You've got to be careful, especially if you haven't got a telly licence, or your leccy's on the fiddle.

WHAT TO PACK?

*D*on't arrive with a bin liner full of dirty washing and say to your hostess, 'Shove these in the washing machine for us, will ya?' You're not Les Battersby, you're a woman of quality. It's always advisable to take more clothing than you need.

In fact, take your entire wardrobe, every single stitch of it. You need to be covered for every occasion. Will you be playing tennis? Or going walking? (Unfortunately, they're big on this in the country.) Or even fishing? If so you might need to pack your rubber waders. These will also come in handy if there's a Tory MP at the party and you fancy doing a bit of business. Be prepared for every eventuality!

LUGGAGE

*Y*our luggage says everything about you. I have a twenty-piece monogrammed matching set, including hat box and cabin trunk, in a beautiful faux leopard print. Stylish and elegant, it certainly leaves snotty hotel staff speechless. And it's very handy at airports, as you can't miss it on the carousel.

Toffs tend to go for Louis Vuitton luggage. It's a sort of dark tan with 'LV' stamped all over it. It's certainly not worth the £600 a case costs and you could be mistaken for a Luncheon Voucher rep. However, if you're one of these flashy nouveau riche types and your heart is set on a bit of Louis Vuitton, then why not spend the money on a holiday in Thailand? You can pick up a bit of Louis for less than a tenner in Patpong market, and it looks like the real McCoy!

GIFTS

You really should take your hostess a small gift as a thank you. It doesn't have to be wildly extravagant. Use your imagination. Here are some suitable ideas:

CHOCOLATE

A box of Roses is okay, but why not go one better? Buy a slab of personalised chocolate from Thornton's Chocolate Cabin. It comes in a very expensive-looking presentation box, and it will delight your hostess.

FLORAL TRIBUTE

A house plant is always an acceptable gift. So how about a nice healthy marijauna plant? Lovely to look at and even nicer to smoke. As an amusing touch, attach a packet of king-size Rizlas to the pot with a lazzy band.

SOMETHING FOR THE HOUSE

Next time you're down the market keep your eye out for one of those dolls in period costume. They look perfect on the sideboard of a stately home. They're not cheap! Expect to pay about fifteen quid for a decent one. I'm very proud of my own collection of Franklin Mint dolls. I keep them in a display cabinet in the lounge, and they are the envy of all my friends and neighbours.

My pride and joy is 'Sarah', a Victorian beauty with a porcelain face and real (well, real-ish) hair. She's dressed in a red velvet crinoline and bonnet, and in her tiny hand she's clutching her tiny muff, perfect in every detail.

ARRIVAL

You'll be expected to arrive in good time for dinner on the Friday evening, so be punctual. Get there about ten in the morning, or even late Thursday night. This will give you plenty of time to prepare for dinner.

It's normal practice to sort out your own travel arrangements. I would suggest that you motor down with your maid and chauffeur. Our Jason usually drives me in something he's hot-wired, and I take our Vera as my personal lady's maid. Christ knows why – she can't dress herself, let alone me, but it looks good to have your staff. Plus Vera really looks forward to a weekend at Lady J's. She was born to a life of domestic service, our Vera. She feels totally at home in the black frock and lace pinny of servitude. Her favourite TV programme was Upstairs, Downstairs. She felt a great affinity with Ruby the scullery maid and used to sit under the kitchen sink chanting 'Yes, Mrs Bridges' like a mantra every time she'd watched it. As soon as we arrive at 'The Hall' she scuttles behind that green baize door and is below stairs to ingratiate herself with the staff like a rat down a sewer. Ladies' maids are usually from France. I've tried to encourage her to act French, y'know, not having a bath and being extremely rude. I've even called her 'Veronique L'Homme de Fromage' to enhance the illusion, but our Vera can't carry it off. She's about as Parisian as a Manx cat.

DRESSING FOR DINNER

A woman should always dress to gain maximum attention, and a lavish dinner party is the perfect occasion to doll up in your best glad rags. For a formal dinner I always say you can't go wrong with black. It looks good on a woman of any age, although fat women are under the misconception that black is slimming. I hate to shatter any illusions, but you can't hide that big arse, whatever colour you fatties wear! Never mind, disguise it with a bustle, or wear a cloak. Forget about your bum and pay attention to your other assets.

Got a big pair of knockers? Then stop moaning about how heavy they are, or how you would kill for a bust reduction, and use 'em to your advantage. Never underestimate the power of a magnificent bosom. Stick 'em out. God gave you that magnificent pair of bazookas to display to the world, not to hide behind baggy sweaters. Be proud of 'em, girl! Wear a daring low-cut frock and watch the effect your heaving bosom has on men.

Enhance your wonderful décolletage with a hint of blusher, and a beauty spot placed on the fleshiest part will enhance your bountiful mammaries. Your skinny, flat-chested sisters will be green with envy and will probably make snide and disparaging remarks about your ample charms. Ignore 'em, jealous bitches. However, if you do have a bust like two aspirins on an ironing board, don't despair. With the aid of a Wonderbra and a clean pair of your old man's socks – hey presto! Eat your heart out, Chesty Morgan.

At the last big function I attended I wore a full-length, backless, bugle-beaded evening gown, slit to the hip with a plunging neckline to the waist, long black evening gloves and a monkey fur stole lined in fake zebra. People stared open-mouthed!

You too can do the same. Be inventive. Show off your individuality. Whatever your size, go for it. Look at Anne Widdecombe. She might have a pudding-basin hair-do and the face and body of a Romanian weightlifter, but she scrubs up nicely. She's never let obesity get in her way.

Hosiery should be sheer and black, seamed at the back with a diamanté motif on the heel. (These are known as divorcee's tights on the Wirral.) A black garter trimmed with red lace is acceptable.

SHOES

Black patent leather stilettos are the only suitable footwear for an ensemble as elegant as yours. So many foolish women ruin an outfit by wearing the wrong shoes. Never, and I repeat, never wear anything lower than a four-inch heel. Flats are out! 'But stilettos ruin the parquet flooring and give you varicose veins,' I hear you cry. Tough! I don't care how big that bunion is, or how painful your corns are – cram 'em into a decent pair of stilies. You'll be glad you did. Think of those poor Chinese women who used to bind up their feet. They suffered for beauty, even if it did make their feet all yellow and curly like Quavers. Don't even dream of shuffling down for dinner in your slippers 'for comfort's sake'. And no, no, no, to Doc Martens. I don't care what Janet Street-Porter wears with an evening gown. Her feet are destroyed from all that walking so she has an excuse. It's just not chic to wear flats. Even my Dr Scholl's have a four-inch heel.

JEWELLERY

Don't wear a ring on every finger. It just looks common. Unless of course it's a State occasion, when you will be expected to wear all your tom. Emulate the Queen Mother and wear two rings on every finger (including thumbs). She can't lift her arms to wave, because her hands are so heavy. She just nods, or maybe that's because all that booze has made her drowsy.

Your wedding ring, engagement ring, eternity ring, plus a couple of sovereigns and a madonna are quite sufficient. You can go mad with bracelets. Wrist to elbow diamanté bangles look sensational against long black evening gloves, which should be velvet or leather. If your arms are bare, cover them in gold. Charm bracelets, gate bracelets, bangles, jangly things – go mad! They look sensational against a sunburnt arm.

The sky's the limit when it comes to necklaces. An enormous rope of pearls hanging down your bare back or wrapped around your neck repeatedly in the style of an African tribeswoman is most effective. It'll hide any lovebites too! (But it can be a bugger to unwind when you're getting undressed for bed, especially if you're pissed). Strands of gold chains, sapphires, rubies, real or paste – it's up to you. There's no such thing as 'too much!' Earrings should be worn big and loud and follow the general theme of the rest of your jewellery.

NAILS

If you're not wearing gloves, then pay attention to your nails. There's no excuse for bitten, broken, plain disgusting nails. Invest in some nail extensions at a salon. You'll have Fu Manchu-length talons in minutes! You won't be able to wash a dish or knit by hand anymore, but why the hell would you want to? Knitting belongs in an occupational therapy class. As for washing dishes, isn't that why you had children? Wiping your bum can be a bit of a hazard with two-inch nails, though – buy quilted toilet tissue and go carefully!

Nails should always be lacquered a deep crimson. Why not try 'Jugular', a deep red nail polish from the Flame of Llandudno collection.

HAIR

If it's long wear your hair up, the higher the better. Like a Maori's hut as me mother used to say. Once your coif is styled exactly as you want, spray it with a can of hair lacquer and then go over it with a hairdryer. It sets like a crash-helmet and shouldn't budge, even if you fall into a hedge drunk.

ACCESSORIES

You're only going down for dinner, so in this instance you only need a small evening purse, big enough to hold your fags, lighter, breath freshener, clean drawers, Mace spray, diary, pen, lipstick, powder, hair lacquer and St Christopher medallion. As for an evening wrap to throw over your shoulders, how about a full-length cape covered in heavily scented orchids? Or an all-enveloping mink or silver fox stole? A shawl can look very effective, providing it reeks of glamour and doesn't look like it just fell off the back of a mill girl. Lush velvet in a deep midnight blue studded with tiny pearls and diamanté is the type of shawl you should be looking at. Trim the ends with the beaded fringing, but be careful if you're planning to go for a drive after dinner in an open-topped sports car, as you don't want to do an Isadora.

Feather boas are an anathema to me. If you insist on wearing one, make sure it's at least twelve-foot long and six-foot deep, with heavy tassles at either end to give extra weight. The feathers should be premium quality, rich and glossy. Black cock feathers are best, long and slightly curled at the end with an iridescent green sheen, similar to what you get on a slice of roast beef. Personally I'd leave the feathers on the chicken. They should only be worn by drag queens impersonating Shirley Bassey. Those fecky department store boas moult. The dye runs and they are nothing more than a bit of string with a few old feathers, plucked from some poor dying turkey's arse, glued on. Well, what do you expect for £7.99?

MAKING AN ENTRANCE

Always be the last to arrive for dinner. Make sure all the other guests are seated. Never apologise. A woman like you never needs an explanation. You will have missed out on the pre-dinner cocktails, but isn't that why you packed a bottle of whisky? There's often dangerous chit chat at a cocktail party that could get you into trouble. . . . For example, if you were asked, 'Have you been to the ENO lately?' what would you say? They don't mean the ear, nose and throat department of the local hospital. They are referring to opera – so best avoid the cocktail party.

Before you go into dinner, get the butler to announce you, for example, 'Ladies and

gentlemen, (pause) Miss (pause) Lily (pause and drum roll) SAVAGE!' Hold back a minute and then slowly and dramatically make your entrance. Imagine an orchestra with lots of brass and percussion playing a strip version of 'Wild Thing, I think I love you'. Move slowly and confidently. Find your light, pause and then say seductively, 'How's it goin'?' Your fellow diners will sit gob-smacked.

Let one of the flunkeys guide you to your seat. Wait till he pulls your chair back and then sit (but make sure the flunkey has moved the chair under you, as don't want to hit the deck, do you?)

The cutlery is a piece of piss – start on the outside and work your way in. There are numerous forks, but don't be fazed. The forks can come in very handy if the old chap next to you puts his hand on your knee.

CONVERSATION

Keep it flowing! Make it light and gay! For example: 'Did you hear about poor Henry at the Royal Academy Summer Exhibition? My dear, he collapsed as he was scrutinising that recently discovered Modigliani. Quite frightful, suspected heart attack.' Or: 'I'm an honorary guest of the Royal Corinthian Club at Cowes this season. Are you?' If the person to whom you're addressing this bit of patter replies in the negative, simply say, 'Really,' and turn away.

THINGS NOT TO SAY OVER DINNER

Don't say:

● 'Our Vera's piles are back.'
● 'Did you know asparagus makes your piss yellow?'
● 'Is this wine Lambrusco?'

Talking with your mouth full of food is de rigueur at a society dinner – they all do it – so throw your head back and laugh hysterically revealing the contents of your gob to the entire table. Spray a few dukes and earls with your food. Spit it all over them – they love it! You'll look like one of the privileged classes.

PETS

Shouldn't be taken into dinner as a rule, especially in Japan, where they will mistake your lovely little shit-tzu for the main course and eat it. However a small garter snake coiled around your wrist or nestling in the warmth of your bosom makes a wonderful conversation piece.

ELBOWS

Unless you're an American, putting your elbows on the table shows a distinct lack of breeding. It should never be done while you're eating. However it is perfectly acceptable between courses if you are talking to the person opposite. Lean forward, elbows on table, chin gently resting on the back of your hand. This shows you are fascinated by the shite he is boring you to death with.

NAPKINS

At a posh dinner you will find a beautiful linen napkin folded into some intricate design waiting on your plate. Don't be impressed. Make no reference to it. Don't turn to the rest of the dinner table and say, 'Have you seen this? Aren't they clever. It's a shame to unwrap it.' Ignore it, it's only a fuckin' napkin. Merely flick it open with your right hand and lay it across your lap.

Don't put it on your head later when you've had a few drinks and sing 'Sally', pretending to be Gracie Fields.

Don't hold it up in front of your face yashmak fashion and flirt with the host's brother by batting your eyelashes. It doesn't look cute, and it isn't clever.

Don't tuck it in your shirt front or blouse unless you're making a statement about being Northern or from Essex.

Don't call them serviettes!

FINGERBOWLS

You may see a small bowl of water with a slice of lemon in it. Don't drink it! This is not an aperitif, it's a finger bowl. It is to be used if one has eaten a dish with one's fingers. Delicately splash your fingers in it, then wipe them with your napkin. There's no need to get the soap and the nailbrush out.

EATING WITH FINGERS

Soup should never be eaten with the fingers, neither should mashed potatoes. Asparagus can be eaten with the fingers – pick up the end of the stalk, dip the head in the hollandaise and lower slowly into your mouth – ideal if you're flirting with someone. You can stare at them as you're doing this, slowly sucking on the asparagus. Finish it off with a wink.

Mussels are served in their shells. Pick 'em up and eat with a teaspoon or use the empty shell from the previous mussel, very chic! Makes you look like you eat them all the time.

STAFF

Ignore all staff. Don't be saying please and thank you every time the waiter fills your glass or brings your food. Even if the butler drops dead at your feet, just flick your ash on him and ignore him. This goes for fancy restaurants as well. If you're ever in a posh restaurant and the snotty French waiter tries to make you feel small, smirking and sneering every time you ask for something, simply say, 'I'm not the twat working for ninety pence an hour plus tips – you are. Now fuck off and get me an ashtray like the good little domestic servant that you really are.' As he swishes off to the kitchen drop your napkin on the floor. Click your fingers and say, 'Boy, I appear to have dropped my napkin.' As he bends over to retrieve it, give him a good hard shove with your foot so he loses his balance and falls over. You can then:

❖ **throw a glass of brandy over him and set him on fire. Or**

❖ **throw a glass of brandy over him and call the manager exclaiming, 'A member of your staff appears to be drunk. This is unforgivable. I shall inform Fay Maschler, well-known restaurant critic and dear chum of mine, who will expose this restaurant as the overpriced, jumped-up greasy spoon caff it is. Furthermore, I have no intention of paying for the regurgitated contents of a sick cat's bowel that you laughingly call nouvelle cuisine. Now fuck off and bring me a bottle of free bubbly and an ashtray.' This usually does the trick.**

BOOZE

*Y*ou will be served: a light amontillado sherry with your turtle soup; champagne with oysters; a good burgundy wine with your main course; dessert wines; liqueurs; port etc. It's a real piss-up at a fancy dinner party, so pace yourself and don't end up blind drunk by the second course. You'll only

disgrace yourself by turning to the Bishop of Wakefield and offering to get your tits out, or asking an MP if he'd like a quick ham shank under the table. Both will accept, so avoid.

When the dinner has ended you usually adjourn to the drawing room (pronounced 'rhum') for coffee and liqueurs. Never call it the lounge or front room. Only the working classes have these.

If you need a wee, then excuse yourself and leave the room discreetly. It's considered the height of bad manners to stand up and announce that you 'need a slash'. The gentry never call the bog anything but the lavatory, so don't say bathroom, loo, toilet or the unforgivable, 'little girl's room'. In fact, don't say anything. Just go.

CARDS

Bridge is the usual after-dinner game. It's a bit boring, so why not suggest a game of poker or Strip Jack Naked?

BEDTIME

If you're going to sleep with one of your fellow guests, then be discreet. Remember, no lovebites! Don't be tempted to dust your bosom or cheeks with a bit of glitter as it's the biggest give-away to who shagged who last night so. It sticks to everything. Lady Ponsonby-Twat might want to know why Lord Ponsonby-Twat is shimmering like a stripper's G-string next morning at breakfast.

BREAKFAST

A good house guest never makes an appearance before lunchtime. A light breakfast can be brought to your room

by your maid if you so require, but on no account should you bounce down the stairs at seven a.m. asking, 'What's for breakfast? I could eat a horse.' Your hostess will hate you. Stay in your room, recover from your hangover, have a bath, do your make-up, prepare for the day ahead. Perhaps you can go for a stroll in the grounds but do not shag the gardener. This is considered very poor taste. No matter how attractive he is.

AFTERNOON TEA

An elegant and graceful affair, served in the afternoon before a roaring fire, which is a bit uncomfortable on a roasting June day. At a proper, full-blown drawing-room tea you can expect to be served vol au vents, sandwiches, scones with clotted cream and jam, sponge cake, chocolate eclairs, ices, crumpets and Indian and China tea. So you'd best smoke a joint in your room beforehand so you can get the munchies.

When pouring tea, never put the milk in the cup first. Only the working classes do that. The milk goes in last. And never drink your tea from your saucer if it's too hot.

Don't peel the sarnies open to have a look at what's in them. I'll tell you now – cucumber, salmon, or egg and cress. To be honest, they're so small they're not worth bothering with. A cucumber sarnie consists of a translucent slice of cucumber between two wafer-thin slices of bread. It'll be about the size of a stamp, so you'll need to shove about ten in your gob at once to get a decent mouthful. Leave 'em alone and wire into a decent slice of cake instead. Which, by the way, is eaten off a plate with a fork.

After tea one can retire to one's room until the pre-dinner cocktail, when the whole thing starts again.

THE HUNT

Some weekend country parties have a hunt. I never get involved in these and neither should you. It really is time they were abolished. If they want to hunt something, then why not chase a couple of football hooligans with a pack of hounds, instead of hunting some poor old fox? Hunters are mad. I mean, the hounds are never called dogs. You can't whistle at them or give them sweets, as they are not pets. Never say to the master of the hounds, 'are you in charge of the dogs, love?' And your beautiful red hunting jacket is not red, it's pink. Don't ask me why the aristocracy say red is pink. Must have something to do with in-breeding.

The only good thing about hunting is the outfit you get to wear. There's nothing to stop you wearing one though … as you nobble the hunt.

There's no need to stand in the middle of Chipping Norton in a kagoule with a banner saying 'Ban Hunting'. This isn't going to save the fox and it gives the gentry something to sneer at as they ride past. Try a far more subtle approach to sabotaging the hunt. Find out its route and position yourself in a field just off the main track. When the horn is sounded, blow the trumpet you had concealed in your knitting bag. This will confuse the hounds. Each time the master of the hunt blows his, you blow yours – the dogs will go demented. The hunt will be called off. The fox will live another day. And you didn't have to wear a kagoule.

LEAVING

Never overstay your welcome. A good house guest knows when to leave. That's why Australians are never asked back. A weekend to an Australian means six months. Just as 'Can I use your phone to make a quick call?' means two hours to Canberra.

Make sure you leave your room in a reasonable condition. Hide any fag burns in the carpet by moving furniture. Remove all empty bottles, coffee cups, empty fag packets, etc. Chuck 'em out the window into the moat. That goes for cutlery and oil paintings as well.

Thank your hostess graciously. Give her a kiss on either cheek and whisper 'Ciao' in her ear. Resist the temptation to pop that diamond earring in your mouth. Tip the butler (a quid should do it) and leave.

You've been the perfect house guest.

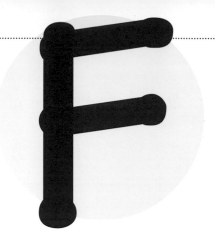

FAIRGROUNDS

I love fairgrounds, especially the smaller travelling ones. I love the music , the various smells, but most of all, the rides. You can hear me screaming 'Give us a push lad' for miles when I'm being spun on the waltzers by a strapping youth with tattoos and an earring, and I always go on the Bobby Horses – I know it's ridiculous – a woman of my age on a carousel but when I hear that Wurlitzer I'm Doris Day in Jumbo.

Our Vera's natural grandmother used to run a fairground. She was a pure Romany Gypsy with the gift of second sight. People ask me if Vera has inherited her grandmother's talents. Can she see into the future? She can't see into the bloody bathroom mirror, I don't know about the gift of second sight. She wasn't particularly blessed with the gift of first sight. Her glasses are like re-entry shields.

FEMINISM

I know that most men have the idea that feminists have facial hair and hairy armpits, and wear dungarees and pit boots. The Alf Garnetts of the world like to peddle this image to keep their 'birds' slaving over a hot stove and looking after a house full of screaming kids whilst they go out and supp their ale. But when I bumped into Germaine Greer at the BBC tea bar she told me what I'd suspected for years – I am a perfect example of modern feminism. Of course I follow the rules of the Elsie Tanner School of Childcare: when it all gets too much have the little sods taken into care and pick `em up four years later. I've never washed a dish in my life, nor let a man order me about. If I want to stay in bed all day, I do, and although they've given me corns the size of golfballs, I wear six-inch-high heels because they make me feel good. Similarly my short skirts are practical for keeping my gusset aired and are nothing to do with showing off my long, much admired legs to every passing male.

Feminism killed off the age of chivalry. A man no longer holds a door open for a lady in case he's accused of being a sexist pig. I was knocked unconscious in the Army and Navy Stores. I was following a bloke out the shop and, being an old-fashioned gal, I thought he may have held the door open for me … WRONG! He let it go straight in my face. I was sprawled out sparko right underneath the Clinique counter.

I don't approve of 'going Dutch' either. If a fellah asks you out to the pictures and a meal, then he pays the bill. This crap about a woman paying her own way to prove that she's independent and no man's plaything wasn't thought up by a feminist. It was thought up by a bloke! Of course it was – think about it! You go to the cinema with a bloke – you pay. You go for a meal – you pay. And then afterwards he gets a free shag chucked in. Well, he's on to a winner, isn't he? No girls, when a bloke takes you out, leave your purse at home – make him pay.

LIVERPOOL STADIUM

WRESTLING TONIGHT

Hell Cat Savage vs The Wigan Mauler

FOOTBALL

An activity that provides highly lucrative employment for hyperviolent males with limited intelligence, involving no more than running around a field scantily clad and attempting to kick a ball into a net. It's usually enjoyed by pot-bellied psychopaths. I'm sure there are some very nice ordinary football fans,

but all the ones I see on telly chucking bottles at foreign coppers are ugly fat pigs.

Apparently there's a big problem with football hooligans. Well, I have the solution. Before the game starts, march all the yobs on to the pitch and then release the lions (not the emblem on a t-shirt, the real McCoy). After the lions have torn 'em to shreds, the game can commence. Great, eh! Gives a bit more value for that extortionate ticket price.

As you've probably gathered, I hate football. Hate, loathe and detest everything to do with it. I get really pissed off when they reschedule my favourite programmes to accommodate a football match. The times I've set the video to tape Corrie only to come home to find I've got Arsenal vs. Liverpool instead of Barlow vs. Baldwin. It makes me so mad I could drown kittens.

If they just showed the match I probably could handle it, but the game is followed by an hour-long post-mortem, where a couple of sporting know-alls and that bloke who advertises crisps give us the benefit of their wisdom.

This still isn't enough. News At Ten then devotes half the programme to the soddin' game. Earthquake in Japan? Never mind that – what about that penalty kick?

Don't go away, there's more to come. After the news stay tuned for a bitingly witty quiz game jam-packed with topical football gags, hosted, just for a change, by Nick Wancock and some middle-class softies masquerading as laddish stand-ups. Hilarious!

Footballers always seem to marry bimbos don't they? Second-rate television presenters who pose misty-eyed with their spouses on the cover of Hello! one minute and then black-eyed and battered on the front page of the Sun the next.

Not all footballers batter the women in their lives, but it's okay if they do. They won't lose their sponsorship or be kicked off the team, because in the religion that is football these men are saints and nothing can touch them. Just say you're sorry in the pages of a tabloid and it's all forgotten.

Drugs are a different matter. The player caught with cocaine will have to book into a rehab centre, flagellate himself in the media and go on a tour of schools as a warning to would-be drug abusers. Then they're forgiven.

A lot of these footballers look dead glam, but let's be honest, they're as thick as two short planks. David Beckham is a stunner, but have you heard him in an interview? Please, he's just a simple lad, don't ask him any hard questions. But who cares when you look like that? There's no need for conversation. All that fuss when he wore his sarong on holiday. I thought he looked gorgeous. No need for the press to take pics the way they did. Jealousy you see – 98% of the press (women and men) would look like ten pound of shit in a two-pound bag if they wore a sarong.

I wrote a song for the World Cup anthem but it was rejected, probably because there are too many lyrics for the fans to try and remember. Let's face it, most fans can't remember what a toilet is. That's why they use doorways. They have the attention span of a goldfish – once around the bowl and they've forgotten. 'Vindaloo' is a much easier lyric for them to get their mouths around. Well, it's the soccer yob's staple diet, isn't it? Apparently 'Three Lions' was equally easy to commit to memory – well,
Skinner and Baddiel seemed to manage it …

Here's my song anyway …

I'm absolutely crazy about David Beckham,
There ain't a woman in the country who doesn't want to neck him.
I've offered him a life of sex, drugs and vice,
But he doesn't want to know,
Because he's goin' with Posh Spice.

CHORUS
Get your bits out for the girls, David Beckham,
Get your bits out for the girls, watch us wreck 'em,
Lay your knob against my thigh,
And I'm yours until I die,
All we want to do is shag you, David Beckham!!

FENG SHUI
The latest craze from Japan that involves moving your furniture around to create a harmonious atmosphere. Your chi has got to be able to flow through your legs and up through your head, and you've got to watch your yin and yang, otherwise it flies straight out the window and then you've had it.

The placing of your furniture should make you feel happy and comfortable so I've had the cooker, fridge and telly put in the bedroom – now I can fry a bit of bacon for me breakfast, watch GMTV without having to get out of bed. You couldn't find a more comfortable arrangement! Well, I'm happy.

FEET
Apart from testicles, feet have got to be the ugliest part of anyone's body. Foot fetishism isn't for me. Nothing would induce me to suck a big toe, not even cash up front. I can't bear anyone touching my feet. Our Vera's got a thing about feet. Her own are actually quite remarkable. They're webbed. She might not be able to wear flip flops but she's a demon in the swimming pool. Her nickname was 'Kipper' at school, 'Kipper Cheeseman', because she spent so long in the water her skin went leathery and turned a funny colour. Her bedroom's crammed with rosettes and cups – mementos of her school days when she won every swimming gala. I remember the Birkenhead News calling her 'Kipper Cheeseman the Toxteth Torpedo' after she'd cleaned up at yet another swimming event. She really comes alive, Vera, when she's submerged underwater. I'm the opposite. I hate public swimming pools. I'm not getting in water that's had all sorts of men, women and kids in it. God knows what you might catch. I went to the baths once and I caught an infection. It was a . . well, never mind – let's call it a women's complaint. I took myself to the doc. 'Does your urine burn?' he asked. 'Don't know,' I replied, 'I've never put a match to it.'

FAIRY TALES

The Brothers Grimm were aptly named. Fairy tales are definitely not suitable for children or impressionable adults. Tales of necrophilia, bestiality, rape, incest, child abuse or sadomasochism with a moral – it's a bit like reading the Sunday Mirror, really.

Take Snow White – yeah, take her far into the forest and bring her heart back, preferably still warm and pumping. My sympathies definitely lie with the Queen. A woman unjustly accused of evil just because she fought her corner.

Imagine you are the most beautiful, drop-dead gorgeous woman in the land, your beauty is unsurpassed. You have wealth, power, a title (royalty no less) and then along comes your 16-year-old raven-headed, voluptuous, simpering little bitch of a step-daughter and steals your thunder. What do you do? Sit back and wait for your cheek bones to cave in and watch Princess Pushy take over? Or practise a bit of self-preservation?

She did right to take action – her only mistake was allowing a man to do the job. That huntsman was a wanker. One look into Snowy's pert little tits and he lost his bottle. If you want a job doing, do it yourself. That brave woman went out in public without any beauty aids and wearing rags to make sure the job was done properly. She failed in the end but it took seven men to defeat her. Brave unsung heroine that she was.

As for Snow White, her choice in men left a lot to be desired. The one she ended up with was a necrophiliac. He only fancied her because he thought she was dead. Well, I suppose that's royalty for you.

FAMILY

I spent a fascinating afternoon at Somerset House researching the Savage family tree. In fact the information that I uncovered is of such important historical interest that my next project is a piece of non-fiction in 15 volumes retracing the Savages from the 1700s to the present day. I will not attempt to tell the Savage saga here as it is a complex skein of wool that requires some time to unravel. However I will do my best with a short potted version, trying to include major historical events and omitting the trivia.

The Birkenhead of the 1800s was not the lively metropolis it is today. If you were to go back through the mists of time in a tardis you would discover a tiny fishing village consisting of a few crofts and the odd isolated farmhouse, 14 pubs, a chippy and a betting office. On the top of the Hill of Birkenhead watching over the sleepy village stood the Convent of the Order of the Most Pious Sisters of Misery, a holy order of nuns dedicated to a life of isolation and self-mortification.

And it was to this grim fortress that Margaret Mary Savage, my great-great-great-grandmother, delivered her beautiful but wayward daughter Kathleen into the care of the nuns. Margaret Mary – or Meg as she was known by the clientele of the gentlemen's drinking clubs across the water in Liverpool – had done very nicely for herself. The youngest son of one of Liverpool's oldest aristocratic families had put young Meg in the family way. Poor Meg knew that an unmarried lass who fell from the path had only one way of supporting herself and that was to join the rank of the many prostitutes who plied their trade along the Dock Road. However since she'd been on the batter for the last two years anyway, she opted for a bit of blackmail to secure the funds a mother and her fatherless child required. The father was a worthless rake, a young buck who used his family's vast wealth and position to get whatever he wanted.

He was betrothed to the daughter of Lord Hooton, a powerful and wealthy landowner, and it was on the morning of the wedding that a vengeful Meg executed her plan. She ran down the aisle of the Birkenhead Priory screaming like a tortured banshee and hit the groom over the head with a shovel.

'I am with child,' she shouted

at the stunned congregation from the altar steps. 'This wedding cannot take place for I am carrying my Lord's bastard child in my belly.'

She turned to Lord Hooton declaring 'Wouldst thou let thy daughter marry a whoremonger, well wouldst thou?'

The marriage was postponed and, to keep Meg from pacing up and down the busy market streets of Liverpool with a hoarding revealing not only the identity of her child's father but his penis size, a handsome settlement was made.

With her new found fortune, Meg bought herself a townhouse, got herself a maid, hung a red lantern in the window and opened shop. She became the proprietress of her own 'Salon des Artistes'. For the entertainment of the salon's male patrons, a tableau vivant would be performed representing great scenes from famous works of art.

Meg, naked but for a length of gossamer silk draped across her beautiful body, would pose, surrounded by a group of scantily clad maidens, as Aphrodite triumphing over Psyche, an appropriate choice in the circumstances. The pièce de resistance was the finale, when two great papier mâché oyster shells would open and inside, representing the pearl, was a naked Meg.

Is it surprising that men fought duels over her or ran away to sea to try to forget about their broken hearts? Meg would give private displays to the discerning and wealthy gentlemen in her opulent bedroom. French was ten guineas and Full Personal Service thirty.

Meg's notoriety

spread far and wide, earning her the title 'The Bawd of Birkenhead'. Her daughter Kitty meanwhile was quietly blossoming into a raving beauty. She was a wilful, precocious girl, and would sneak downstairs to her mother's salon and flirt with the customers. Her youth and beauty were the perfect wine to honey the jaded aristocratic palate. Meg was having none of it and banged her sexually precocious 16-year-old into a nunnery.

The young Kitty stood in front of the mother Abbess, a raw-boned giantess with hands like shovels and size twelve feet and felt sick. Blessed Mother Arsenius stared down her long nose at Kitty and sniffed.

'So, Kathleen Savage, do you think you are worthy to enter a life of pain and suffering, of prayer and penitence, of chastity? Do you want to become a bride of Christ?'

Young Kitty chewed her lip and gave the matter some thought. Eventually she said, 'I'd rather have a long engagement first.'

Of course young Kitty never took the veil and the nuns, in desperation, sold her into a life of domestic service as a maid of all work in the South African mining town of Kimberley.

Hopeful diamond prospectors poured into town and headed for the only hostelry, the Hard Times Saloon, to find a bed. The proprietress of the Hard Times was a Dutch

immigrant called Mrs Van de Morrison and she realised that in a town full of thirsty men a beautiful face and body behind a bar can help sell a lot of drink.

As well as serving ale, Kitty would dance on the bar counter and sing simple folk songs for the men :

You've been rootin' around
In a hole 'neath the ground
Searching for Mother Earth's treasures.
She'll never reveal 'em
She knows that you'll steal 'em
She'll surrender her pearls at her leisure
I'm keeping my baubles hidden away
Keeping them safe till Mr Right comes my way
He may be a pauper, he may be an Earl
He'll have to dig a little harder, for
He claims my pearl.
My beautiful opals
Are the finest in the land
Milky white
A pure delight
Would you like to hold one in your hand?
My seam's staying closed
Until you've proposed
These gems are inviting
They sparkle and shine
But you aint gonna see 'em
If I close down my mine.
Oh yes I'm keeping my baubles hidden away
Until the right man comes along.

The prospectors would go berserk! Cash poured into the tills. The shrewd Mrs Van de Morrison realised that she had a gold mine of her own in the shape of young Kitty and she made her a partner in the business. You can't keep a good Savage down. If we fell off the roof of the Co-op we'd come up with the divvy.

But something happened – a dirty great hairy-arsed bluebottle fell in the ointment. His name was Davey O'Brien, a young Irish prospector. He wooed the lovely Kitty. He wooed her morning, noon and night, wooed the arse off her he did. Inevitably all this wooing around put Kitty in the family way.

A mining town was no place to bring up a baby. Davey had offered to marry Kitty and spare her the shame of single parenthood, but she turned him down. Looking after a baby was hard enough without having to look after a husband as well.

She had to get away from Kimberley, but where could she run to? Dame fate smiled upon Kitty because that morning she received a letter from a firm of Liverpool solicitors informing her that her mother, the infamous Bawd of Birkenhead, had died leaving her townhouse and 200 guineas in her will to Kitty. A week later Kitty set sail for Liverpool from Cape Town.

Kitty gave birth to a beautiful girl whom she christened Zinnia after the exotic flower. Young Davey made a fortune in the diamond rush of 1871. He returned to Ireland a wealthy man but died a pauper ten years later, his fortune squandered on the gambling tables. All that remained was a single uncut diamond that his daughter later travelled to Ireland to claim. The further adventures of Kitty will be revealed in my forthcoming The Savage Saga.

Zinnia Bernadette Savage had inherited her mother's good looks but she was also her father's daughter. Zinnia was uncontrollable; a spitting, hissing, feral animal who cared for nothing but gambling, drink and men. At pontoon and poker she always cleared the table, in a drinking bout she was indefatigable and would drink the hardened drinkers under the table. She swore like a pirate, fought like a Kowloon Docker yet she was a passionate woman who had many affairs that she tossed aside like an old glove when she tired of them. Was there no-one capable of taming her wild spirit? It didn't seem like there was, but then one day, at a horse fair, she met the man who would change her life. She needed a new horse. A wild stallion, 19-and-a-half hands high, a vicious, snorting powerful beast with a wild eye and a thirst for blood was led into the auction arena. Eight men were needed to restrain him.

Zinnia knew that here was a kindred spirit. She bought him and insisted that she ride him home. The horse was having none of it. Zinnia put up a brave fight but was eventually thrown from the monster's back and kicked in the head. She was taken to the caravan of a travelling Patent Medicine Man. His name was Liam Rouke, the seventh son of a seventh son. The caravan shook from their wooing over the next four years. Zinnia bore him four daughters.

War had been declared, Zinnia returned to Birkenhead, her lover took the King's shilling and joined the Army. The night he was posted to the Western Front Zinnia gave birth to a daughter. She was born on the eve of All Hallows as the church clock struck twelve. A shadow crossed over the moon and dogs went crazy in the street. Hecate Savage was born.

Liam returned to Birkenhead three times during the war. The second daughter was born at exactly the same time as Hecate was. A black cat howled at the moon from the sill outside the infant's window and a mole bit a dog on

a nearby farm. Cattermole had arrived.

The third child, another girl, was born in exactly the same circumstances but this child was different from her sisters. Her hair was not the hue of spun silver, it was fiery red. The colour of her father's hair. She was named Verbena.

The last child was born on a bright August morning, no dogs howled, no crops failed. Zinnia went into labour at a tea dance for service men's widows. After a very short uncomplicated labour she gave birth to Erica in the Ladies' cloakroom. Outside the band played 'Aufwiedersen'. Little Erica's first words were 'Give me a cigawette'.

Erica grew into a beautiful young woman. Bored with Birkenhead she hitched a lift on board a merchant ship bound for Bremerhaven. From there she travelled to Berlin. It was impossible to gain employment as a cabaret singer in pre-war Berlin. Frightfully decadent English gels were all the rage. Erica, even though she was from Birkenhead, looked more Teutonic than Sauerkraut.

Sat in a Russian tea shop off the Kurfurstendam, one afternoon, a young girl struck up a conversation with her. She was fascinated by the world weary Erica, her hooded eyes, her magnificent bone structure. The blonde hair that hung over one eye and the languid way she smoked a cigarette were to influence this young girl for ever.

'What's your name kid?' Erica asked.

'My name is Marlene', the young girl replied. 'Marlene Dietrich and I want to be a film star'.

Granny Erica always claimed that Marlene had nicked her

screen persona from her. She modelled herself on my grandmother even down to the way she spoke. Granny hated her for it. The name Dietrich was never allowed to be spoken in her presence.

Erica got a job singing at a club called 'Der Blau Blitzkreig'. One evening she caught the eye of a very prominent visitor. He was bewitched by this little bird and invited her to spend the weekend at his mountain retreat hideaway. Granny declined on this occasion for she had other things on her mind, but she was always the sort of girl who knew on which side her bread was buttered and so when the invitation was repeated she accepted. Granny often spoke of her stay at

Unity Mitford, a woman she was later to describe as 'weally fwiendly'. The host was none other than Adolf Hitler himself.

My grandmother was later accused of being responsible for starting World War Two. She has always maintained her innocence. To her credit she did valuable work for the resistance, risking her life on numerous occasions. After a series of hair-raising adventures she returned to Birkenhead via the Isle of Man bringing back her six-month-old daughter, Violet, my mother.

My mother grew up to be one of the greatest female wrestlers ever, 'Hellcat Savage The Wirral Wildcat'. She reigned as Queen of the ring for eight years, only to be defeated by the underhand and unprofessional tactics of a dog called the Wigan Mauler. After her retirement my mother became an odour eater demonstrator for selected chain stores up and down the country.

I was born on 14 June, 19 er can't remember, on a policeman's overcoat outside the Legs O'Man public house, Lime street, Liverpool. My adopted sister Vera arrived three months later. My story requires more than a few pages to do it justice, but my autobiography, which I am currently writing, comes out next year.

FINLAND

I worked in Finland once. It's populated by alcoholics, who, if they don't commit suicide, opt for a career in dentistry. They also eat reindeer, have sallow complexions and have no sense of humour whatsoever. Finland – what a depressing hole. I'd sooner chew me own nipple off without an anaesthetic than set foot in friggin' Finland again.

GUILT

I gave up guilt years ago. The lesson to remember is: if it's going to make you feel guilty then don't do it. If you're one of those people who lies awake at night eaten alive with guilt and remorse because you absent-mindedly popped a grape in your mouth while you were browsing around the fruit section in Tesco's, then don't even think of going behind your best mate's back and sleeping with her husband while she's at work, as you certainly won't be able to handle the aftermath. The trouble with you is you're a decent human being. An honest and upright citizen incapable of straying from the path of righteousness without that conscience of yours getting the hair vest and flagellation kit out. (See also under: Wimp, Creep, Goody Fucking Two Shoes).

The Catholic Church perfected guilt. As soon as you hit seven they have you in that confessional singing like a canary to the parish priest. How serious can the so-called sin of a seven-year old be? What could a kid of that tender age do that was so bad? On second thoughts, these days. . . . When I went to confession I used to invent sins for the benefit of the priest. Well, my childish sins seemed boring and I didn't want to let Cannon Kelly, our nice old priest, down so I'd make 'em up (which of course is a sin in itself and a sin that was never confessed either, thus defeating the whole bloody object). He must have got really bored listening to children's confessions, so instead of 'Forgive me, Father, for I have sinned – I stole a sweet from the pick 'n' mix' or 'I forgot to make my bed,' I'd give him 'Forgive me, Father, but I've murdered me mother, had sex with his Satanic Majesty and burned my sister alive.' It used to brighten his day up.

'That child needs a team of exorcists working through the night, not a simple priest like meself!' he'd say to my Mam. Happy days!

But back to guilt. Forbidden fruit is always the tastiest but always gives the worst gut ache, so from shoplifting to sleeping around, if you're not the kind of hard-faced bitch who can pee in a swimming pool without flinching, leave it to the experts.

Glamour

Glamour …
Could make a Ladye seem a Knight
A nutshell seem a gilded barge,
A shelling seem a palace large
And youth seem age and age seem
*   youth*
All was delusion, nought was truth.

'The Lay of the Last Minstrel' –
by Sir Walter Scott

I couldn't have put it better meself. The word 'glamour' originates from the World of Faerie (see Witchcraft). The Fairy Folk would deceive foolish mortals by 'casting the glamour o'er them'. This powerful spell would bewitch men's senses, making them see something that wasn't there. Gypsies, fairies and witches had this power – a little sprinkle of the old glamour dust and a hideous old crone could be perceived as a devastating beauty. Our Vera would sell her soul for a drop of faerie glamour. She'd need a couple of gallons, though, for it to have any effect.

In the 1930s Hollywood adopted the word glamour to describe the sultry sirens of the silver screen – Garbo, Harlow, Dietrich – these names are synonomous with glamour. Bewitching beauties that women (and some men) tried to emulate.

Anyone can be glamorous. It's all about physical allure, it's a state of mind. You could look like Bill Sykes's dog, but with the right attitude, cleverly applied warpaint and discreet lighting, you can be transformed into a smouldering vamp. After all, Marlene Dietrich was just plain old Maria Magdalene Dietrich, a plump teenager with mousey hair, until Max Factor and Josef von Sternberg got their hands on her.

So go on, treat yourself. Throw away the flannelette nighties and slip into an oyster satin chemise instead. Soak yourself in Chanel No. 5 and recline seductively on a leopard skin chaise longue (if you haven't got a chaise then the bed will do) and indulge in a box of sinfully decadent Belgian Truffles and a bottle of Dom Perignon. Think glamorous, feel it oozing from every pore – you should be so hot you could fry an egg on your thigh, sssssssss. . . . A life without glamour is not worth living.

GILES

Never trust a man called Giles. Particularly those who talk loudly on mobile phones.

GYMS

I've been to a gym twice. The first time I did the weights – the bench press, the treadmill, the exercise bike – you name it, I went on it. I came out two hours later, glowing. I was in bed for the next two days unable to move a muscle, in total agony. Friends, who attend a gym regularly, told me that I'd done too much too quickly, and that I should get a personal trainer. I thought that only police dogs had them. But apparently if you're a gym virgin you need someone in a leotard to supervise you, so I got one. I had hoped he'd be like one of the masseurs you see in Dallas – tall, square-jawed, a heaving rock-hard mass of muscle, who didn't mind where he put his strong hands. But Ron, my personal trainer, was a short, balding, slightly plump youth in black lycra, which made his arse look like two black puddings. 'Oh well', I thought, 'C'est la vie....' He put me through an hour of 'gentle' exercise which he must've learnt from the Gestapo Handbook of Extracting Information and for which I shelled out £35. As I was leaving the gym he shouted after me 'Don't forget, in the morning do ten crunches'. So I did. I lay in bed and ate them. Honest to God, I genuinely thought he said 'Crunchies' – anyway I'm not paying to be tortured again, so sod him. I'm quite fit enough.

GOATEES

A goatee should only be seen on Jimmy Hill, Acker Bilk and certain breeds of dog.

They look hideous on anybody else. Shave it off!

GOOD-TIME GIRL

An old fashioned expression, quite often used in a derogatory fashion to describe a woman with a sociable nature who enjoys life to the full.

Some of us were born with the words 'Good-Time Gal' running through us like the letters in a stick of rock. It's in the genes, and it's not our fault if we prefer sitting in the pub to housework.

While it's frowned upon to be a G.T.G., it's very fashionable to be a 'ladette'. Zoe Ball and Denise van Outen are typical ladettes, although how either of 'em manage to have a good time when they both have to be up at the crack of dawn for breakfast shows is beyond me. Maybe they go to afternoon tea parties and get slaughtered instead of all-night raves.

The Patron Saint of the Good-Time Gal was Elsie Tanner, a woman who was glamorous, tough and not afraid to use her potent brand of sexuality to get her own way with fellahs. Poor old Elsie always backed a loser when it came to men. These bastards would invariably shit on our Else from a great height but, undaunted and ever optimistic, she would dust herself down, slap the warpaint on and head for the Rovers. 'Flamin' men – give us a gin, Betty.'

Of course where there's an Elsie you'll find an Ena. There's always some foul-minded,

moralising old nit ready to wag the finger and spread a bit of juicy gossip – I had one living next door to me. Her name was Kathleen Kelly. I can say what I like about Kathleen on these pages. There's no danger of her suing 'cos unless the library stock this book in large print she won't be reading it. Kathleen was a wizened old skeleton with a tongue like a viper. The woman was evil personified. The numbers 666 were burned into her forehead and I had regular run-ins with the wicked old bitch.

She'd lurk behind her net curtains and as soon as she saw me coming

down the landing she would appear on her front doorstep on the pretext that she was putting the empty milk bottles out.

'You're late home,' she said to me one night, as I was coming home from the Hot Voodoo Club.

'Us artistes of the theatre keep late hours, Mrs Kelly,' I explained. 'What's your excuse?'

'I'm awake because the noise of those bloody stilettos clacking down the street would wake the dead,' she hissed. 'I'll have to take a Temazepam now to get off.'

'Why not take the whole bottle?' I asked in a neighbourly fashion. 'Wash 'em down with a bottle of Scotch, then turn the gas on.'

She surveyed me through gimlet eyes.

'Artiste was it?' she said. 'Like Michaelangelo? You've a lot in common you two, both spent the best part of your working life flat on your backs – whore of Babylon.'

She slammed her front door in my face before I could think of a suitable reply.

'That's right – get back into your coffin before the sun rises,' I shouted through the letterbox. A bit feeble, but then I had been working all night, so give me a break.

I used to get this sort of abuse all the time. Kathleen always called me the whore of Babylon. It was grossly unfair – Lloret de Mar maybe, but I haven't even been to Babylon.

TO BE A FULL-BLOODED DYED-IN-THE-WOOL GOOD TIME GIRL IT'S HANDY IF YOU...

✔ **Are a divorcee.**
✔ Wear too much make up.
✔ **Sleep in your make up.**
✔ Have big hair.
✔ **Dye big hair.**
✔ Drink gin, brandy and Babycham, Tia Maria, and Yate's white wine.
✔ **Eat prawn cocktails, steak and chips and Black Forest Gateau in a Berni Inn.**
✔ Wear an ankle bracelet.
✔ **Sport an all-year-round sunbed tan.**
✔ Smoke like a chimney.
✔ **Leave lipstick smudges on cigarettes, stamps, glasses and tea cups.**
✔ First thing you do in the morning is look in a mirror and say 'Gawd almighty you look rough.'
✔ **Second thing you do in the morning is look in your handbag for fags.**
✔ Run out of fags.
✔ **Eat at Le Pont de la Tour restaurant with flashy**

middle-aged men from Essex who wear more gold jewellery than you.
✔ Be the first on the dance floor.
✔ **Slow dance to 'Lady in Red.'**
✔ Know every man in your local.
✔ **Have more men friends than women.**
✔ Be the life and soul of an Anne Summers party.
✔ **Have a 'well wisher' send social services round to check up on your kids.**
✔ Wear a black bra and let the strap show.
✔ **Wear a black bri-nylon underslip in bed.**
✔ Find yourself crying at three in the morning.
✔ **Wear high heels – always.**
✔ Wear black tights, summer and winter.
✔ **Show lots of cleavage.**
✔ Be on a permanent diet.
✔ **Have a shoulder to cry on.**

✔ Show great resilience in the face of adversity.
✔ **Have a knee trembler in a back alley.**
✔ Be seen in kebab shops, Taxi ranks and at the back of night buses attwo in the morning.
✔ **Know the words to 'Y Viva España'.**
✔ Have at least two Tom Jones and a Shirley Bassey LP in your record collection.
✔ **Paint your toenails red.**
✔ Say 'I'm finished with men' at least once a week.
✔ **Go on ladies' nights and help the male stripper take his G-string off.**
✔ Always have a supply of condoms in your handbag.
✔ **Own a snow-washed denim skirt.**
✔ Be permanently skint.
✔ **Be optimistic.**

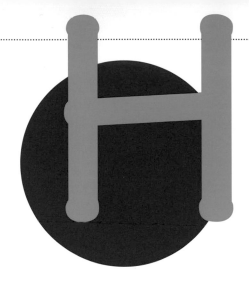

HARRODS

Reputed to be the most famous shop in the world. I beg to disagree. I'd say that KwikSave has a higher profile.

Harrods is a fabulous shop but it also has the rudest security guards in the world. Put a man in a uniform, even if it is slate-grey flares and white socks and the megalomaniac in him takes over.

Me and my beautiful family were refused entry into Harrods, can you believe it? We had popped over to Knightsbridge one Saturday to do a little 'browsing'. We hadn't set foot inside the door when we were pounced on by a gobshite in uniform.

'We have a strict door policy at Harrods'.

'I'm glad to hear it,' I said.

He sneered, and continued, 'And you are not entering the premises with that.' 'That' was a tiny little rucksack our Bunty was wearing over her shoulder. They are the height of fashion these days, everyone knows that, apart from Harrods security.

Our Jason got it next.

'We do not allow members of the public into the building wearing torn clothing,' he said nodding at our Jason's jeans. Our Jason's not one to piss about when it comes to standing up for himself.

'What are you on about, man?' he said. 'These kecks are cool, one-side arsehole.' I did try to explain that our Jason's jeans were Jean Paul Gaultier and that the rips were actually very expensive rips, but my mobile phone went off mid-flow.

'I'm sorry madam, but if you want to use that then you must get back on the streets, Harrods … '

'Yeah, I know, doesn't permit the use of mobile phones in this jumped-up fucking shop. It's not the Vatican y'know,' I said and nutted him.

We didn't get in, so we went home and came back dressed as Arab women. He didn't recognise us and he let us in, bowing and scraping this time. We had a lovely time, we robbed the place blind. Serves 'em right.

HEALTH FOODS

The best six doctors anywhere
Are sunshine, water, rest and air,
And exercise and diet.
These six will gladly you attend
If only you are willing.
Your ills they'll mend
Your cares they'll tend
And charge you not a shilling.

I've got serious doubts about the benefits of vitamin pills and a diet of organic veg and wholefoods – the people who swear by this diet are certainly no advertisement for it. Go into a health food shop and have a look at the person behind the counter. They look like they've been dug up and hit with the shovel. The same goes for those filthy new age hippies who flog organic fruit and veg at trendy markets. Pale and wan, they stagger around behind their stalls weak with exhaustion through lack of proper nourishment. A pan of mince would kill 'em. I don't know how anyone could become a vegan, nothing would induce me to eat a bowl of pulses, or tofu. Apparently if you fry it, tofu tastes like bacon – what's the point? If you crave the taste of bacon then have bacon – slap a nice big thick rasher in the frying pan, not something that looks like a yeast infection. I've got to be honest – if it hasn't looked over a hedge I don't want to know.

HICCUPS

The best cure for hiccups is to swallow a teaspoon of vinegar – handy if you have an attack in the pub that docs scampi and chips 'cos you'll always find a bottle of Sarson's on the bar.

HYPOCHONDRIA

If you ever ring me at home and our Vera answers the phone then for God's sake don't greet her with a cheery 'Hello, how are you?' as she will tell you – a long, drawn out, boring account about the terrible condition of her poor bowels. 'How are you?' is a salutation, a rhetorical question, but not for our Vera. She takes it literally and for her it's an open invitation to indulge in her favourite topic of conversation – her health, and how ill she is.

You see, my sister is a chronic hypochondriac. There's one in every family, but when it comes to whinging about her ailments, our Vera is the Queen Bee. The Reader's Digest Medical Dictionary is her Bible and there isn't a pill or a potion that she hasn't sampled. Vera's bedside cabinet looks like Boots the Chemist – it's her favourite shop and she spends many a happy hour cruising the aisles testing what's on offer – not lippy or perfume like other women, but cough medicine and indigestion tablets.

For her, ill health is something to celebrate. She's as happy as a pig in shit when she catches a cold. It gives her a legitimate excuse to take to her bed and hide under the duvet with her torch, poring over her medical dictionary to see if her symptoms match those of double pneumonia, which of course they invariably do. No common virus would dare to land on our Vera, oh, no no no – only the virus with a pedigree infects that one's bloodstream. Indigestion becomes E. coli, a headache is a brain haemorrhage, and it's a great day in the Cheeseman household when her pile comes back. She's only got the one apparently but how she looks forward to the home coming of the haemorrhoid, the Return of the Prodigal Pile. I can always tell. The bathroom is littered with suppositories and pile preparations. I cleaned my teeth with a tube of 'Preparation H' once, mistaking it for Signal. Disgusting. She's the High Priestess of the Patent Medicine worshipping at the altar of SuperDrug, forever going about her business with Vicks Sinex rammed up her nose and a suppository rammed up her arse. Once, after she'd consumed six Beecham's powders and a bottle of Night Nurse, she got a bit confused and put the wrong one in the wrong hole. The suppository did nothing for her sinus but the Vicks certainly gave her pile a bit of a tingle. Her underwear drawer stunk of menthol for weeks. She's proud of her pile – out comes the much repaired inflatable rubber ring so she can sit down and watch Emmerdale in comfort. In the ad break, she implores me through quivering lips and a martyred expression to 'Ring the doctor, Lily, I'm in agony'. The kids roar laughing, because to be honest she's really quite comical when she's in this state. 'You've no idea what excruciating pain a pile can be', she says, bristling with indignation. 'I bear my pain in silence, and all you lot can do is laugh. You won't be laughing when me haemorrhoid haemorrhages and I'm stiff on a slab in the morgue.' Wincing with the imaginary pain, she gets the aerosol can of 'Spray'em and Shrink'em' out of her knitting bag and quotes the blurb on the back of the can like a mantra:

'A doctor should be consulted when any of the following conditions are present: intestinal obstruction, symptoms of appendicitis, acute abdominal pain, nausea, blood in the stool or vomiting.'

It puts me off me tea.

'I've got all those symptoms, Lily', she raves. 'Ring an ambulance, I'm dying.' She seems to confuse the ambulance service with 'Dial A Ride'. She'd have them take her shopping if she could wangle it. The kids laugh even louder especially when she tells our Jason to put the sidecar on his motorbike to take her to casualty. 'I might just be able to make it to the hozzy in that', she says in a weedy voice. 'If I put me rubber ring on the seat and you drive slowly and don't go over cobbles!' We do have a laugh with her. She's good value for money. She was the same when she was a girl, and while she wasn't the prettiest girl in the school (to be brutally frank, she's very plain our Vera) she kept herself clean, was a champion knitter and was the life and soul of every party. You could always rely on Ve to liven a 'do' up. After a few bevvies, she'd strip down to her vest, play 'I'm just wild about Harry' on her harmonica

and do a bit of Irish dancing to entertain us. Oh yes, they certainly broke the mould when they made Vera. So what turned this lively young gal into a ball of misery? I blame men for the transformation in our Vera. She's been let down badly a couple of times in the past you see. We don't talk about it in front of her, she refers to it as 'my great tragedy' (see V for Vera).

She went downhill after 'her great tragedy', seeking solace in the bottle and numbing her tortured mind with hard drugs.

It was an awful period, she'd drink anything (still does) that made her high. I once caught her putting Brasso in her Horlicks. Her days were spent in a drug-induced haze, her weekly giro was handed over to a shifty youth who provided her with the necessities to get her into her required state. Cocaine and quaaludes were her favourites, especially the coke. She was forever annoying the dentist and her favourite tv programme was What's My Line?. I remember how disappointed she was when she discovered that line dancing didn't involve a mirror and a rolled up five pound note.

Thankfully, she's calmed down. She's not quite as bad as that now, we still have to watch her though, as she's inclined to squirt Mr Muscle Oven Cleaner up her nose if she isn't supervised. These days she's addicted to disease. Our poor doctor is demented. She's never away from his surgery. In the end to shut her up he put her in hospital for observation and there were 300 doctors a day at least who queued up to peer at her through the big glass window of the observation ward. She'd lie back wanly, a lilac chiffon scarf wrapped around her head like ectoplasm and half a pot of dead white face powder on her papery cheeks making her look more like a corpse than ever while the medical experts prodded and poked her. It was the happiest time of her life.

The specialists could find nothing wrong with her but to keep her happy they gave her lots of pills as a placebo.

'Do you know what, Lily?', she told me proudly one visiting day, 'I'm so ill they're giving me tablets made out of that stuff that babies live off in the womb.' She even had a brain scan but they found nothing. 'I've got fusions on the brain', she'd croak, perched on top of a bedpan. 'Me poor brain has fused like a 13 amp plug!'

They sent her home in the end much to her disgust but it didn't stop her thinking that she had some terrible terminal illness that the medical profession hadn't yet recognised, yet alone been able to diagnose and treat.

She's more to be pitied than censured. I told her to stop thinking about herself all the time and get out the house more, meet people, broaden her horizons, and if she tidied herself up she might get herself a fellah.

A fashion accessory to our Vera is a surgical collar, an eyepatch, slings, tubigrips and catheters, and where most women would prefer a pair of pearl and diamond clips to adorn their ears, our Vera opts for a pair of cotton wool balls to hang out of her ear'oles – just in case she has a wax discharge. She still can't get the stains out of her cardigan after the last big fall out.

I gave her some of my old things – they were going to the recycling bin anyway, so don't start crediting me with altruistic motives. She never wore any of them even though she looked lovely in the ski pants. Even so – surprise, surprise – she met a fellah. Our Vera is living proof that there is still a chance for those who are plain and over 40 to find lasting happiness and romance. They make a lovely pair, he's got a look of Crippen about him and they do their courting in the council mortuary where he works as an embalmer.

It's funny isn't it? How a punch up the knickers can cheer a gal up. Our Vera hasn't mentioned her bad neck/bowel/ear/back/eye etc since he's been slipping her a portion. Her sexual appetite is voracious and he's on to a winner as the smell of embalming fluid drives her wild. One whiff and she makes him take her right there and then in the middle of the morgue. She always did say she'd end up stiff on a slab in the morgue. She was right.

HAIRY BACKS

Ugh! Disgusting on a man, even worse on a woman.

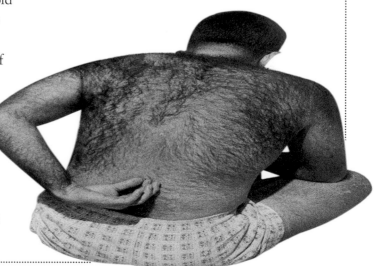

If you've never been stricken by this crippling illness then you shouldn't be reading my book, unless of course you're one of my young readers who has yet to discover the dubious delights of alcohol abuse. How well I remember my first hangover! I was fourteen and still attending St Risley's Secure Unit for Girls. We'd been allowed to stage our own musical for the St Risley's Open Day, attended by senior nuns, pupils' mothers and, for those of us who had 'em, pupils' fathers. There would also be a smattering of social workers and anybody else the nuns of St Risley's could get to sit through one of our amateur performances. This year's show was a moving tribute to Holloway Prison entitled 'Hooray for Holloway'. One of the girls had made some punch to celebrate at the show 'party' (to be held in the laundry cupboard so as not to disturb the sisters).

The recipe for this punch was two bottles of nail varnish remover, as many potato peelings as we could steal from the kitchen undetected, and a can of fluid that was used in the Roneo printing machine. We added two pints of water and left it to steep in a bucket – for a month. This recipe may not sound your cup of tea, but please remember we had no choice. After all, we couldn't just pop out to the offie if we fancied a bevvy, so needs must!

You can imagine what state we were in after we'd drunk this imaginative potion. Matron was furious! I got three days in solitary and privileges suspended for this little contretemps. To tell you the truth I was really grateful to be banged up in the cooler for a few days. Such was the severity of this hangover it was bliss to lie in the dark with nothing to disturb me but the sound of my own erratic breathing and moans of agony. I have never drunk nail varnish remover since!

The hangover is 'The unpleasant after-effect of over-indulgence in alcohol', or so says my copy of Universal Home Nurse and Midwife,

first printed in 1902. A very dismissive way to describe a frequent near-death experience, if you want my opinion. Let me explain it for you – the cause and the treatment of the hangover.

What probably happens is ... you fall into your bed at four in the morning, deliriously happy after an evening's jollification with some dear chums ... only to wake at midday with one side of your body completely paralysed. You may also discover that you are trapped inside the duvet cover. Don't panic! Release yourself from this death-trap and face the day – you will be blinded by the light, as you forgot to draw the curtains last night. You will also be suffocating from heat, as you didn't open the window and you went to bed in all your clothes, complete with faux leopard-skin coat – and guess what today is? The hottest June day on record since the Thames dried up in 1170 and Henry II got heat stroke on a day trip to Canterbury and murdered some fella called Becket in a barny.

You will now try to stand up. That leg of yours is still dead. It's slowly starting to return to the land of the living, and the dull pain in your paralysed limbs is slowly metamorphosing into pins and needles. You hop towards the bathroom, and manage to stand on the up-turned plug of your carelessly flung hairdryer. The pain is agonising, but nothing to compare with the pain that blinding midday sun is giving to your poor sore bloodshot eyes. Bravely you carry on like a wounded animal, seeking the sanctity of a dark bathroom. Standing in the dark, gripping hold of the sink to steady yourself, you allow sufficient time to recover from the journey. Switching on the bathroom cabinet light and peering into its mirror, you try to open your swollen eyelids – no easy task! Your famous Ballet Rouse No. 19 false eyelashes may be long gone but the glue has remained, sealing your lids up like a couple of envelopes. What happens next will come as a terrible shock. You've finally managed to open your eyes and you're looking like the lovechild of Alice Cooper and Edith Piaf. Don't panic! Those deep lines etched around what were once your eyes only look worse, because your eye make-up has run into them, making them stand out more. You'll be okay after a good wash. Yes, I know it's heartbreaking to see a head of hair that ten hours earlier was a highly commented-on, gravity-defying mass of fascinating curls tumbled, and now sadly a shadow of its former glory. Don't panic! That wadge of embedded chewing gum will eventually come out.

HELPFUL HINT Stick your head in the freezer compartment of your fridge until the chewy has gone stiff. You'll be able to break it off quite easily after it's frozen. If your freezer box is too small to take your head, then try lying in a chest freezer. But do tell a member of your family or the supermarket staff, in case you nod off.

Assessing the damage and having got over the shock, you will probably start to experience a feeling of self-loathing and mentally flagellate yourself.

'Never again!' you will moan. 'Why do I do it?' Because you're a social animal, that's why.

Any attempts to purge yourself by cleaning your teeth will result in a severe bout of dry retching. If you cannot control this quickly enough, the retching will undoubtedly bring on wet-retching, 'the real McCoy' (as you will call it later on during a telephone conversation to one of your fellow sufferers), 'vomiting your ring up'. Depending on what you had or didn't have for supper, severe stomach pains may occur, followed by an unexpected bout of diarrhoea. Don't dawdle! Rip off that roll-on quickly! And hit that lav.

If the diarrhoea and vomiting occur at the same time, you will find it convenient if your bathroom sink is in close proximity to your lav. Projectile vomiting of the Exorcist variety is the worst. It will force you to improvise. The sponge bag containing all your make-up is a big no, and so is the bath. You will only have to deal with it later. Believe you me, this is a big job and not one for the squeamish. They should make people doing community service come round to clean it up for you; that would teach them to mug old women. Try to open your legs and force your head between them, into the lav, while you're sitting there – this is the most practical solution.

After the vomiting has subsided you will sit there, on that lav, blowing your nose on a bit of toilet paper, your body racked with pain, and you will go into self-reproach mode, feeling old, tired and pathetic. You need to return to the bedroom quickly and bury yourself back under the safety of the duvet. This symptom is called 'seeking the security of a womb substitute' by American experts. Bollocks! It's called going back to bed. Aren't some American doctors twats?

On your return to the solace of your boudoir, be prepared to encounter one of the following in your bed:

(A) An ashtray, complete with ten days' worth of stumps, that has somehow made its way in the night from your bedside locker to the middle of the mattress.

(B) A half-eaten doner-kebab.

(C) A carton of Kentucky Fried Chicken.

(D) A traffic cone.

(E) A carrier bag you've never seen before containing sick.

(F) A strange man.

(G) A strange woman.

(H) Both of the above.

(I) A giant cockroach listening to his Walkman on the headphones. (This means you are probably experiencing the delirium tremens. If it's not the DTs then you will need to phone the council; either way, you need to seek professional help.)

If on returning to your bed you find that (F) or (G) have occurred then do the 'Christ Almighty, look at the time, I'm late for work/my husband/wife will be home from work any minute', act. Just get rid of them. If they refuse to move, cut their throats and bury them under the patio. Nothing pisses a girl off more than a shag who hangs about.

Hopefully, though, there will be no nasty surprises waiting for you and you can lie peacefully under your duvet. Your head will be throbbing. The back of your throat and your nose will be sore from the vomiting and there will be a strange heaving and rasping sound which will be your lungs after two hundred fags in the pub last night.

Don't even bother trying to recall the events of the previous evening as you will soon start to have flashbacks of a woman with no blouse on singing 'These Boots Are Made For Walking' at

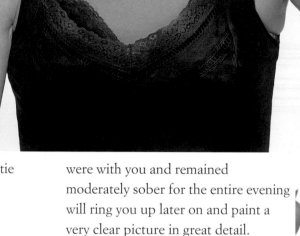

the karaoke night in a public house. Hopefully that drunken trollop wasn't you! There's a good chance that the woman who told the young lad who collects the glasses to 'get his dick out' and give his auntie 'a lick' wasn't you either.

Never worry. If you have no recall at all about the night's events, those friends who were with you and remained moderately sober for the entire evening will ring you up later on and paint a very clear picture in great detail.

THERE ARE VARIOUS CURES FOR THE HANGOVER

1 The Prairie Oyster This is a disgusting concoction of Worcestershire sauce, Tabasco, raw egg, tomato juice, vodka and Christ knows what else. It is usually taken by the upper classes, but then most of them are masochists anyway, thanks to the public school system.

2 Hair of the Dog This may cure you, or it may just top up the alcohol level in your blood and give you a taste for the ale again. That 'Hair of the Dog' could turn into a kennel full of Pit Bulls.

3 Black Coffee A bit strong, I always find, and it can act as a laxative which is the last thing you want if you've already got the Bombay Crud. The only advantage is the caffeine rush, but then you can achieve this from twenty Pro-plus and a cup of tea – far more civilised.

4 Drinking Water Before Retiring Ridiculous even to suggest this, because you'll never remember – and who the fuck is capable of drinking any more liquid?

HELL RAISERS

A select band of highly revered men, usually film stars or footballers who occasionally turn up on chat shows, either blind drunk or half alive, shaking from the DTs, and bore us to death with that tired old tale of how they went on a 48-hour drinking binge in Italy with Ollie and then smashed up the hotel bar.

It amazes me how these bleary eyed, physical wrecks can recall these benders with such clarity. Every conversation is remembered word for word. Every date, every detail, and yet they claim that their lives have been spent in an alcoholic stupor. If I've had a bevvy I can't remember me own name yet alone who I punched in 1971. Makes me suspect that the majority of the Hell Raisers' stories are pure fabrication, figments of their imagination. The only incident that they can't remember is the time when they beat their eighth wife up in a drunken rage. They put this amnesia down to a 'black out' as in 'I woke up next day and couldn't remember a thing, my mind musta gone blank. I didn't even know I'd hit her till I found her front teeth embedded in my knuckles'.

Hell Raisers can be identified on chat shows because they are the only people who are allowed to smoke. The older ones would put you off fags for life. Their coughs sound like the death rattle of a consumptive walrus, they drop ash on their clothes, their fingers are bony and black with nicotine, their nails are long and yellow. The entire body trembles. They sit cross-legged in the unfamiliar chair listening to Parky's question, wiping phlegm from the mouth with a handkerchief after one of these coughing bouts. Makes me want to give up. If these people weren't famous then 'Hell Raiser' would not be a term that was applicable to them – they would be classed as your common or garden, brainless yob, and I suppose, with the exception of the great Brendan Behan, that's all they are.

Women who are hell raisers are looked upon differently from the men. A young hell raiser is a 'wildchild' – she hangs around bands and pop stars, goes to every party, wears outrageous clothes (ie, next to nothing), she always has her picture in the tabloids and she gets her tits out at the pop of a flashbulb. She might get a job presenting a hip late night music programme, interviewing a gang of girls out of their minds on 'E' in the Glitz night-club in Doncaster. After shagging half the music industry and two football teams she'll have a short stormy marriage to a pop star ending in either a messy divorce or a messy death when hubby chokes on his own vomit after a massive heroin overdose. If the 'wildchild' is an addict herself then she may attempt to take her own life and be incarcerated in a drying-out clinic – the correct behaviour for a pop star's slutty wife.

Another route is home to Mum. The tabloids love this, it shows contrition. She's learned the error of her ways – no more drugs and parties for her. She's staying with Mum in Croydon and might even develop bulimia. If she makes the mistake of trying to get on with her life and continues to socialise, maintaining a high profile, then the tabloids will crucify her. She has not served a respectable period of mourning and the harlot must be stoned.

Paula Yates should have been born a man – she would've been hailed as a hero for the way she's lived her life. Paula is guilty of nothing more than gross vulgarity. She does not deserve the ridicule and abuse that the media dole out to her on a daily basis. I was shocked by the cruel reaction of the press when she tried to commit suicide. Like jackals with smell of blood in their nostrils they went for her throat, the bitch of the species tearing into the Yates carcass with a ferocity that left the males way behind.

This species is known as the 'columnist', a coven of self-opinionated, frustrated bitches who delight in venting their poisonous spleens on any poor bastard who steps out of line. They vie for the title 'the first lady of Fleet Street'. The Queen of the Witches, old mother Rook, is long dead. Her Ruby slippers lie empty, waiting to be filled. Roll up! Roll up! Ye foul minded hags, which one of you is worthy to wear the crown?

Poor old Paula was crucified and not one of them showed an ounce of sympathy. Her attempted suicide was just another 'selfish' blot on the Paula Yates copybook. She cared nothing that her children would be left motherless, she was a disgrace to motherhood, unnatural, cold and she must be driven into the wilderness. As you read the sanctimonious drivel that these women think passes for constructive journalism, you can almost hear their bosoms rising with self-righteous indignation. The maternal instinct flowed with the venom in their veins and spilled out onto the page. The truth is that if any of these dogs ever dropped a litter they would probably eat it alive.

Say what you like about Paula, but she loves her kids and she must have been in a pretty desperate state to do what she did – give the girl a break!

Oh no, Paula left her husband, ran off with a pop star, had her boobs lifted, pouted in little girl frocks, called her children by ridiculous names – she deserves it. The only tone of regret in their articles was that she didn't succeed in topping herself.

Listen if I found out that Hughie Green was my natural father I'd be rushing up to the bathroom to find a razor blade as well.

Courtney Love was a hell raiser, but she got her act together and stepped from the pages of Rolling Stone to Hello!

Marianne Faithfull is the ultimate in hell raising. What she hasn't done isn't worth talking about. When she sings the songs of Brecht and Kurt Weill you believe her because you know she's been there. I want to be Marianne Faithfull when I grow up.

HOTELS

The majority of hotels in this country are overpriced slop houses. I hate it when I have to stay in a hotel but unfortunately when I'm on tour I've no choice.

I always take my trusty electric frying pan and Baby Belling stove on tour. It means that I can make myself something decent to eat and not have to rely on room service, a euphemism for a slice of processed boiled ham served between two slices of white bread, bearing the thumb and forefinger prints of the decrepit night porter who made it, garnished with soggy crisps for £4.99.

I have had murder with hotel managers about frying bacon in my room. I've been accused of stinking the corridors out and even of setting the fire alarm off!

D'you know that sign that reads 'Please Do Not Disturb' that you hang outside your door? Well maybe that's how it reads to you and me, but to a chambermaid's eyes it says 'Please bang on my door hard repeatedly with the Hoover at 7 am until you hear me screaming', and you can bet your sweet arse that the early morning call will be from housekeeping enquiring if you would 'like some clean towels?'. How many towels does a hotel chamberbaid think a single woman needs in a day? Anyone would think I was running a couple of Turkish Bath Houses, or a busy midwifery department. Piss off and let me get my kip.

Dogs are a big no-no in most hotels. Apart from the odd few, a dog is as welcome in a hotel as an animal liberationist in a mink farm. My Buster has glowing references praising his exemplary behaviour as a hotel guest and he doesn't nick towels, complain or abuse the staff, so what's the problem? I'm guilty of all three crimes and more but they let me stay.

I hate patronising staff. The snottiest staff I've ever come across are to be found in one particular hotel in Edinburgh. The receptionist is a jumped up streak of French shit and he deserved the stick that I used to give him. He would look down his superior nose at me as if he had just discovered a turd in his bidet.

It's always customary after an artiste has performed in the theatre to go for a little dwink (as Granny Erica used to say) – when you've just sweated blood and tears you can't expect to go back to the hotel and go to bed, you need to unwind and, apart from the hotel in question, Edinburgh has many hospitable establishments where a gal can enjoy a few beers.

Anyway, after I'd unwound for a few hours I  would return to the hotel in question. A typical conversation might be as follows:

Me: Can I have my key please?

French Twat on Reception: (With his back to me, doing his best to ignore me) Pardon?

Me: My key.

F.T.: (Answering the phone and totally ignoring me until eventually) Room number?(sniff).

Me: 'fraid I can't remember.

F.T.: Name?

Me: Savage.

F.T.: What?

Me: SAVAGE!

F.T.: 'ow you spell it?

Me: S.A.V.A erm G.E

F.T.: (Starts tapping into his computer. After ten minutes he asks.) When did you check in?

Me: Monday.

F.T.: (Silence followed by another ten minute tapping session.)

Me: Look, sunshine, you've seen me around the hotel often enough. You know who I am.

F.T.: (Still tapping, not looking at me.) I don't know who you are or in fact what you are, we have to be careful, we can't allow just anybody into the 'otel.

Me: (Grabbing him by the throat.) Is that so? Well I know what you are and it begins with a C and ends in a T and it isn't Catherine the Great. Now give me the key to my fuckin' room or I'll shove your teeth so far down your throat you'll be eating snails through your arse!

F.T.: Au Secours!

Me: (Shaking him by the throat.) GIVE – ME – MY – FUCKIN' – KEY!! – NOW!!

Suddenly the Assistant Manager arrives on the scene. He's also French.

Ass. Man: Can I 'elp?

Me: (Screaming.) I want my key!

Ass. Man: Room number? (sniff)

Me: (About to spontaneously combust) I can't remember.

Ass. Man: Excusez-moi, Madame? You can't remember?

Me: (Losing plot completely and turning into a borderline psychopath) Where am I? Scotland or the Chans-a-shaggin'-leecee? Listen Marco fuckin' Pierre shite, the reason I can't remember my room number is because I'm pissed and I'm in this condition because I'm paying over a hundred and fifty quid to kip in a miserable shitty little room the likes of which poor Anne Frank and her unfortunate family were incarcerated

before your lot turned them over to the NAZIS (here I get really petty). Maurice Chevalier? Bloody Nazi sympathiser. Now give me the key!

At this point in the procedures, Buster my dog pokes his head out of the holdall I'm carrying and growls.

Ass. Man: Alors! You 'ave a dog?

Me: No, it's a singing fucking kipper.

Ass. Man: A HA! Now I know what was responsible for the mess in the elevator. It was your dog who pee-peed in my elevator!

Me: No, it wasn't my dog that pee-peed in

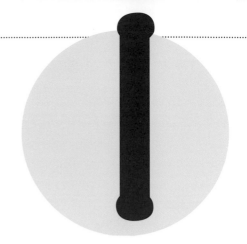

your elevator. It was me.

Ass. Man: Madame, we do not allow dogs in the hotel.

Me: You wha? What about the staff? Some of them would pick up best in breed at Crufts any time. 291! (Suddenly I remember my room number) 219! I mean. (Go behind reception and pick up key myself) Thank you. I'd like my breakfast in my cell at about 11:30 in the morning. Goodnight.

Ass. Man: But what about ze dog!

Me: Oh don't worry about him, he never bothers with breakfast. Just a fag and a saucer of tea. Goodnight.

The lift arrives and thankfully I escape to the Anne Frank Suite. But what a bloody palaver. I hate hotels. I hate the way they fold the end of the lav paper into a point. What's all that about? I hate their continental breakfasts of croissants and coffee, just means they can't get the staff to come in and cook a proper breakfast. Hotel and catering does not pay good wages. Next time I go on tour I'm stopping in a caravan – be a lot easier on the nerves.

USEFUL TIP

Don't steal the towels, dressing gowns and bedding from the hotel room. Take advantage of the unattended maids trolley in the corridor, that way your crime will go undetected. Plates and cutlery can be hoisted from trays left outside other rooms, wash them in the bath.

IRRITATING LITTLE WAYS

Prolonged irritation can drive the victim over the edge into the dark void of insanity and turn them into a gibbering cabbage. Then again they might crack and smash your head in. Here are some wonderful irritating little habits guaranteed to drive people crazy.

- Whistle constantly in the office. Pick a catchy tune from a popular tv commercial. Keep it up all day, you'll find that your colleagues can think of nothing else. They'll even wake up humming the damn thing.

- Sing the first line of a well-known song over and over again until you've implanted it in their brains forever. (Well at least four days.) Watch them go slowly insane until they hear the rest of the lyrics, they'll end up buying the CD so they can exorcise the ghost that is haunting them. If you pick an old obscure song and pretend that you don't know what it's called, your victim will find it hard trying to locate it in HMV.

- If you are in bed with your partner and you can't sleep, then keep 'em awake by asking stupid and meaningless questions like: 'What do you think happens when we die? Is there a God? I think....' And then give them a lengthy theological lecture about life after death. Keep them awake.

- Ask people what star sign they are. When they answer say: 'I thought you were.'
- Tell people what you dreamed last night – remember every single detail.
- Gay men – quote lines from Absolutely Fabulous. Air kiss, say 'sweetie and darling', 'bolly and stolly', laugh affectedly.
- Say 'I bet you were really pretty when you were young.'
- When someone arrives at a party and they've obviously made an effort to look good, greet them with: 'God, you look shattered, sit down.' And, 'Are you OK? You look really ill.'
- Get 'call waiting' on your phone so when you're talking to someone and another call comes in tell them to 'hang on a tick' while you see who it is. Leave them hanging on for at least 10 minutes. If they are still on the line when you get back to them, don't apologise, carry on as if nothing has happened. Ask a casual 'now where were we?'
- Offer an alcoholic pal, who is trying to dry out, a drink. Be persistent, lay it on thick and hard. Describe to them in great detail how a large vodka served with crushed ice, tonic water and a slice of lime tastes.
- Never be on time for anything – always arrive at least 20 minutes late.
- Do a huge pile of washing at home but take it to the local laundrette to dry it. Pick a busy day and commandeer all the tumble dryers.
- Be unable to make a decision. When asked what you would like to do, watch, eat etc. always reply 'Don't know. What do you want to do?' Let others make the decision and then say you don't want to. Don't offer an alternative.
- Buy a female friend or relation, of any age, bath cubes and talc for Christmas. A tiny hankie with their initial on is also guaranteed to piss them off.
- Never carry cigarettes – always bum other people's.
- Never carry matches. Let 'Have you got a light on you?' be permanently on your lips.
- Vanish when it's your turn to buy a round.
- When dining in a restaurant with a group of people, query your share of the bill when it comes to settling up. Nit pick over minor items, get your calculator out and then borrow the money to pay off a pal and then conveniently forget to pay 'em back.
- Smoke a pipe or a really strong cigar in a restaurant, blow smoke towards the next table so the people tucking into their first course get a good blast of Old Holborn with their soup.
- Trap people at parties and display your endless well of knowledge about Dr Who/Star Trek/The Prisoner. Name the episodes, directors, the make-up woman, plot lines etc.
- If you are a teenager or young kid, it will really upset your glamorous, well-preserved 42-year-old auntie if you repeatedly make loud references to her age. Say things like: 'Zoe Ball is ancient – she's at least 22.' 'What did you do in the war?' 'Can I count the lines on your face Auntie?'
- Constantly repeat yourself – drunk or sober.
- Women – act cute and 'girly' in the presence of men.
- Barstaff – when you are giving the customer his change back do so in small coins. Slap it in a puddle of beer on the bar top and then walk away. Watch their fury as they try to retrieve their wet coins.
- Pull the communication cord on packed commuter trains.
- Leave the milk out of the fridge overnight to go off.
- Become a journalist.
- Hog the duvet.

- Leave hairs in the bath.
- Buy a dog that barks all night and leave it chained up in your yard so the neighbours can hear him as well.
- Leave matchboxes full of spent matches lying around. Hide all other means of lighting a fag. Your victim will go mad with frustration every time they try to strike a match.
- Cyclists, ride your bike on the pavement. Remember, roads are for cars, pavements for cyclists, gutters for pedestrians. Scorch towards pensioners at high speed and then at the last minute, swerve to avoid 'em – gives 'em heart failure.
- Stand outside the theatre that is showing Agatha Christie's The Mouse Trap and tell the American tourists who did it as they pour in to see it.
- Never wash up after you.
- Never flush the toilet, and men leave the seat down and pee on it.
- Smoke your mates' fags after they've gone to bed. Don't leave them any for the morning.
- Girls, never have the money ready in shops or when boarding one-man buses. Take your time looking for your purse, hide it at the bottom of your shopping trolley. When you eventually find it, cause more delay by rooting around in your purse for the correct money. Drop it coin by coin into the driver or till girl's hand.
- Give your wife crabs.
- Win every time you play Bingo, turn round and smile at the losers who were waiting for one number. Say 'I've won again' in a smug voice.
- Men, when you shave, leave your filthy water in the sink. Your wife will be unable to have a wash until she braves the cold water covered with a layer of scum and bristle and pulls the plug out.

- Be a very … s.l.o.w. … Bingo caller and when calling numbers out, confuse the women by calling 'On its own number (pause) 32. Those legs (pause) 9.'
- In a supermarket, if you come across a famous person shopping, make sure you talk about them in a loud voice within their earshot. Point them out to other shoppers. Follow them around the aisles and stare rudely. Say things like:

'She's older than she looks on telly.'
'Are they her own teeth?'
'You'd think with the money she's earning she'd make the effort to dress up!'

Grab them at the check out and demand their autograph. Never have a pen or paper. Grab their wrist and cling on with a vice-like grip. Tell them a long boring, drawn out story about how your sister's best friend's husband's mother saw them outside the stage door of a provincial theatre in 1962 and said

'Hello'. Ask if they remember them. Tell them about your ailments. Watch their eyes glaze over. Look at that fixed grin as they desperately try to escape from you without causing offence.

- Cause huge delays at a cash dispenser. Request statements, a printed balance, pretend you're surfing the net, take your time and watch the queue behind you grow longer. Great if it's raining.
- In the rain, carry a huge golf umbrella when you are walking down a busy street. Poke people's eyes out.
- If you drive a one-man bus, then never pull into the kerb when you stop for passengers. Park in the middle of the road and block the traffic. Cause a lengthy traffic jam. Take your time when collecting the fares.
- Play all your flatmates CDs and leave them out of their cases. Dance on them and spill sticky soft drinks over them.
- When you're at a Social Club, play the fruit machine with the £100 prize. Have more than your allotted 'gos' on it. Ignore the irate queue of pensioners behind you and keep feeding the machine until you win. Watch their faces as the coins cascade out of the machine and into your handbag.
- At the supermarket: Take a full trolley to the seven-items-and-under till. By the time the cashier twigs you have more than seven items it will be too late for her to tell you to go to another till. Remove barcodes and prices from merchandise. She'll have no clue to its cost and will have to call a supervisor. Pay by cheque. Take ages to pack your shopping. Watch the faces on the queue behind you.
- Sniff constantly. Especially at meal times. See who cracks first and screams at you to blow your nose.
- Bang on people's doors at 7 am and ask them if they know 'What Jesus said?'
- Wheel a double baby buggy very slowly along a busy, narrow pavement.
- Pepper your speech with phrases like 'Do you know what I mean?', 'At the end of the day,' and 'To cut a long story short.'
- Tear the last page out of the book your friend is reading.
- Constantly recite ad nauseum the details of Monty Python sketches – funny walks, dead parrot sketch – all that old student crap.

- **Become a Street Entertainer.**

IRONING

I'm suspicious of anyone who claims that they enjoy ironing. 'It's so relaxing,' they say. So's lying on the beach at Marbella with a Pina Colada in your hand. Ironing is a miserable way to spend an afternoon. I don't care how fancy your iron is – buy crease-resistant fabrics instead.

JEAN CLAUDE VAN DAMME

Now I know he's only tiny, no bigger than a Borrower, and I'm fully aware that hc comcs from Brussels – a dreary hole where they put mayonnaise on their chips – but what a man! Small but perfectly formed, Jean Claude doesn't seem to have much luck with women. His marriages seem to always end in failure. Why is that we ask ourselves! Because he hasn't met the right woman yet. His last wife complained that he was a bit of a party animal who demanded sex 24 hours a day – what is the woman's problem? You wouldn't hear me complaining – he could take what he likes, help himself. I'd be on call morning, noon and night – I wouldn't even bother getting up. I'd lie in the bed with me nightie round me neck and a dab of scent on me pulse points. So if you're reading this Jean (funny name for a lad) and you're looking for a woman who knows how to have a good time, get yourself on that Eurostar – Momma's waiting!

KISSING

It takes a lot of experience for a girl to kiss like a beginner.

LEGS OF MAN PUBLIC HOUSE, LIME ST., LIVERPOOL.

I was born on a policeman's overcoat outside this famous pub. I had our Jason in the same circumstances. Like a tribal birthing hole, us Savage women return when it's time to give birth. It's been turned into an extension of the Empire Theatre now - shame.

MOVING STATUES

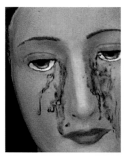

Moving statues are always discovered by a drunk on his or her way home from the pub. In rural Ireland you'll find many little grottoes on the roadside devoted to the Virgin Mary. Inside these grottoes will be a statue of the good woman herself. If you're ten parts pissed, then anything moves if you stare at it for long enough. And I fail to believe that the mother of Jesus Christ – a woman chosen by God to give birth to his son on earth – is going to come back as a £4.99 plaster of Paris statue.

Surely someone with such heavenly special effects at Her disposal would choose something a little more dramatic? Parting the Irish Sea, for instance, and appearing stood in a golden conch surrounded by heavenly bodies? Or racing across the sky in a silver chariot pulled by winged horses with all sorts of cherubims and seraphims kicking up a fuss with bugles and trumpets to announce her arrival? But no. The Mother of God chooses to make her presence known in a damp patch on Mrs Muldoun's back bedroom wall or on the back of a King Edward potato.

I'll have to have a word with the good woman when the time comes for me to meet me maker, let her know how important making a showbiz entrance is. . . .

MR BEAN

Will someone please strangle that gurning moron?

MIXING DRINKS

It's never a good idea to mix your bevvies. You'll only pay for it the next day. So remember, never put whiskey and cider in the same glass – keep 'em separate.

METRIC

Whose bright idea was it to go metric? Grams and kilos and litres and metres. As far as I'm concerned a meter is something you fiddle and I'm fucked if I'm walking a kilometre to the butchers, asking for six grams of corned beef and a litre of milk. No, in our house it's still yards and inches, pounds and ounces, and it always will be. Our Vera never got over decimalisation. She still calls fifty pence ten bob.

MANNING

I was stood outside the Winter Gardens in Blackpool one afternoon, waiting for a pal of mine, when I was approached by what looked like an oversized toad dressed like a darts player. It was the stuff of a child's nightmare, little and fat, with knock knees and podgy hands and fingers adorned with dirty rings. Gimlet eyes, like those of the pigs in The Amityville Horror, peered at me from out of a mass of broken veins and slobbering jowls that could only be described as a face on a coroner's report. The thing leaned forward.

'I've raised a fortune for fuckin' charity, me,' it rasped in a Mancunian accent, 'and you know why folk still pack my club* night after

fucking night eh?! It's because I'm fuckin' funny. Value for money me.'

The creature had been picking its nose while it was delivering this information and it was now looking for somewhere to wipe it. I backed away. He flicked it at a raddled old pigeon mooching around on the pavement and resumed his rant.

'Fucking Ben Elton,' he said. 'What a wanker. I call a spade a spade, me, eh?!' He started to cough and laugh at the same time.

'What do you want?' I said, fed up with this geriatric derelict's rambling. 'If I give you some money for a can of Tennent's Super, will you piss off?'

'Give me money?' he spluttered, his face growing purple. 'I'm a millionaire, ya daft cu . . . ” Fortunately he had another more severe coughing attack and so I missed the last bit.

'Do I know you?' I asked. His face was vaguely familiar.

'Yer wha?!' the eloquent one replied. 'Yer don't know who Bernard Manning is? I'm

* The world-famous Embassy Club. A derelict concrete edifice in the middle of a bombsite on the outskirts of Manchester. Inside is an all-pervading odour of Jeyes fluid and piss. Apart from the obligatory gutter slash curtain you could be in the workhouse from Oliver. The Dickensian material that the proprietor mistakenly delivers as comedy also suits its general ambience.

fucking Bernard Manning!'

'Are you?' I said. 'I hope he's paying you well, because you'd need a strong stomach to shag that ugly old bastard. Mind you, you're no oil painting yourself.' I'd often wondered if Bernard Manning ever got shagged by anyone – animal, vegetable or mineral. I assumed he couldn't find anyone to do it – that's why he'd never married and was so devoted to his mother. No one else would put up with him. Now this thing came along claiming to be Manning's lover.

'What are you fucking on about?' he screamed. 'I'm no fucking pouf! I'm all man, me,' and to confirm it he grabbed – or tried to grab – the region lurking underneath his tenth belly. All I could see was a piss stain in his beige leisure slacks. Suddenly he lurched towards a passing old lady.

''Ere, my love,' he said. 'You know who I am, don't you? Would you like me to slip you a portion?'

Luckily the old lady was one of the good-time granny brigade, dressed in a shell suit with a thirty-bob perm, so she didn't take offence.

''Course I do, Bernard,' she cackled.

'See, everyone knows me,' he said triumphantly. 'Even this daft old bitch.'

'Yes,' she went on. 'We all know Bernard. When you're on a pension you can't afford a turkey. So thank God for Bernard's turkey roll. What was it you used to say on the telly? Bootiful! That was it, wasn't it?'

Bernard hitched his slacks up and stomped off.

'Ta ra Bernard,' the old lady shouted to the retreating blob. 'When are you back on telly? Haven't seen you for years.'

'Fuck off!' was Bernard's only reply.

'Miserable fat sod,' she said to me. 'Where's this portion he promised to slip me?'

MARRIAGE

Why buy a book when you can join the library?

MILLENNIUM DOME

They've built it, now let's see what they're going to put in it. Not that I'm bothered. You won't find me going to Greenwich on New Year's Eve 1999. You can't get a bloody taxi back home!

NAIL BITING

To prevent a child or your sister from biting their nails coat them in an unpleasant tasting substance. Dog shit is an excellent preventative and cheaper than the expensive preparations available on the market.

NOSTALGIA

If you're very old or very lonely then the past is something you cling on to. For any one else, though, to pass your time wishing that life was how it was then, wallowing in nostalgia is an unhealthy state of mind.

Now I might sound like a mean old cow, but I'm serious. Listen. There's nothing wrong with a reminiscing session for a while – that's perfectly acceptable. It's good fun as well. But to do it constantly is sad. In retrospect, the past, to a lot of folk, is always remembered with a rosy glow. They were the best times of your life.

'Times were great then,' you sigh, staring into your glass. 'They really were the good old days.' Well they weren't, they were probably just as shitty as life is now in fact I bet in ten years' time you'll be spouting the same twaddle about today. '1998, life was wonderful then.'

Trying to recall old faces or conversations, the colour of the carpet in your Aunty Mary's parlour, beginning every conversation with 'Do you remember when?' It's a a waste of bloody time. You've got a future ahead of you. Give that more thought instead. 'Onwards and upwards', as some hearty posh sod whose name I can't remember once said.

OLD AGE

'I don't want to grow old', people say. Well you know the alternative.

POLARI

Remember the fabulous Kenneth Williams and Hugh Paddick on the radio programme Round the Horne? I'm glad you do 'cos I don't, I'm far too young. I heard them years later on LP and was fascinated by the language they spoke.

'Oooh' Kenneth Williams would screech, 'How bona to varda your dolly old eek!', which loosely translated means 'How wonderful to see your handsome face.'

This is called 'polari'. A slang that originates way back with the Romany gypsies. They would speak 'polari' amongst themselves so outsiders couldn't understand them. A sort of private code. The acting profession then picked it up (actors will pick anything up) and started to use it and very soon it was adopted by gay men. Palare has more or less died out, any gay man who uses it now is instantly branded an 'old queen'. I use palare, so do Vera and the kids. It comes in very handy sometimes when you don't want some nosey parker to know what you're saying about them. You don't have to be gay, a gypsy, or in the acting profession to speak it, so why not have a go? Bring back polari!

Here is a glossary of terms in polari. There are just loads of words and expressions. Here are just a few:

BONA – wonderful, fabulous, anything that's pleasing.

NAFF – awful, can also mean heterosexual.

MARTINI – fingers

GROYNE – ring (as in jewellery)

BUGLE – nose

SCREECH – mouth – sometimes face.

ECAF, EEK – face

OGLE – eye

OGLE RIAH – eye lashes

PIGS LATTIE – stye (on the eye)

OGLE FAKES – spectacles

JARRIE – food

GOOLIE – black

HOMMIE – man ('H' is silent)

FEELEY HOMMIE – young man

HOMMIE PALONE – effeminate gay man

PALONE – woman

ANTIQUE H.P. – old queen

DELPH or POTS – teeth

LATTIE – house

LATTIE ON WHEELS – caravan

MEASURES/HANDBAG – money

COD – beneath contempt, rubbish, amateur. 'The act was cod' (appalling performance.)

BRANDY – buttocks

CARTES
 – a gentleman's penis and testicles

JUBES – breasts

DASH – leave quickly as in 'dash the lattie' (vacate the premises quickly).

DROGLE – dress or frock

CAMP – anything that is original, unusual, outrageous or amusing. Depends entirely on the individual's taste.

MAQUIAGE/SLAP – make-up

ORDELID – climax

NANTEY – no

VARDA THE NAFF HOMMIE WITH NANTE POTS IN THE CUPBOARD – Look at this unsightly wretch with the appalling dentistry.

VARDA THE GROYNE ON THE ANTIQUE H'S MARTINI! – Look at the size of that ring on that elderly homosexual's hand.

PALARE THE ANTIQUE H. FOR THE BEVOIS. – If you engage our elderly friend in conversation he might stand a round of drinks.

I HAD BONA ARVA OFF THE HOMMIE BACK AT THE LATTIE. – My masculine gentleman friend shagged me senseless in my house.

GET THAT BONA JARRIE DOWN THE SCREECH. – Eat this wonderful food.

VARDA THE CARTES ON THE HOMMIE – Look at the size of the bulge in that man's trousers.

TIPPING THE VELVET/CLEANING THE CAGE OUT – cunnilingus

BATTS – shoes

SCHIKEL – wig

RIAH – hair (spelt backwards)

TODGE H.P. – passive gay man

ARVA – sexual intercourse

COLLISEUM CURTAINS – a big foreskin

QUONGS – testicles

SHARP/LILY LAW – police

LALLYS – legs

VARDA – look

PALARE – talk

TRADE – either sex, or used to describe a man you are having a sexual encounter with.

TRADE – a casual sexual relationship.

AFFAIR – long term partner.

NANTOIS TRADE – I didn't encounter a sexual liaison tonight.

VARDA THE RIAH – look at the state of my hair.

NAFF FEELEY HOMMIE – I'm jealous of that very young man.

GOOLIE OGLE FAKES – sunglasses

✪ Some words can have 'ois' added as in the French. Nante-ois, bev-ois.

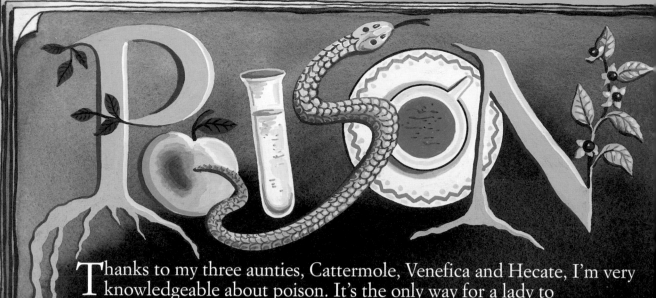

POISON

Thanks to my three aunties, Cattermole, Venefica and Hecate, I'm very knowledgeable about poison. It's the only way for a lady to dispose of her victims. Now while I'm not advocating that you pop a bit of hemlock in your old man's soup, it will do him no harm to let him know that you are familiar with poisons. Make him think twice about giving you a dig in the gob when he's had a bevvy. Poison can be extracted from herbs and plants – grow some in your windowbox or garden. They are very pretty, but for Christ's sake keep the kids and pets away (unless, of course, they're getting on your nerves as well. . . .)

HEMLOCK

This innocent-looking, elegant and graceful plant has delicate white flowers and you'll find it growing all over the place. An Ancient Greek by the name of Socrates was poisoned with it. He was a stand-up comic and if they didn't like your act in those days then there was no getting paid off. The management simply slipped a drop of hemlock in your pint of bitter. A custom that should be brought back – there's a few comics I'd like to see taking their last breath.

It's a bit of a bugger to administer. Cooking destroys it and it stinks like a polecat's hole, so you can't use it raw. Use your initiative! Carve an old-fashioned penny whistle out of the hollow woody stem and present it to the man who's done the wrong – encourage him to try and knock a tune out of it. A few blows on this poisonous pipe, and it's bye bye … You can poison a whole dinner party by making toothpicks out of the stem. When they say that the meal was 'to die for', never was a truer word spoken. The cause of death is suffocation, but you never even had to pick up a pillow.

WOLFSBANE

Also known as aconite or monkshood, and in Scotland referred to as avid wifeshood, Wolfsbane is an easily grown, hardy perennial with exotic dark blue and purple flowers. It's very pretty

and looks lovely growing along your borders. Wolfsbane is a virulently poisonous plant – one of the best! Supposedly, if you wrap the seeds in a lizard skin and carry them in your handbag it allows you to become invisible at will. Grow a tub outside your front door – it will protect you from vampires, werewolves and television licence men. The root of the plant is deadly, pop it in a pan of scouse. Or how about a few leaves in a ham salad sandwich? Wolfsbane is also used in the making of love potions. But be very careful. One drop too many and you've got a stiff on your hands, rather than a stiffie in your hand.

As in most poisons, the cause of death is suffocation. That's after they've writhed around the kitchen floor in agony with a numb tongue and an unbearable itching sensation all over their body for half an hour. The only antidote for this deadliest of poisons is tincture of digitalis (foxglove).

berry was once used by Liz the First to give her eyes brilliancy. A tiny drop causes the pupil to dilate. Like self-abuse, too much can make you blind. I expect Liz the Second uses Eye Dew like the rest of us.

A few berries tossed in a fresh fruit salad will go undetected. Your victim's hands will twitch, their eyes glow like hot coals and slowly they will suffocate to death. Beats hacking him to death with an ice-pick, and there's no mess.

If it's taken accidentally then you'll need to administer an emetic (not to be confused with an enema). A glass of warm vinegar taken internally will cure 'em.

DEADLY NIGHTSHADE (BELLADONNA)

Easy to grow, liking chalky soil and shade, the Devil's own plant has beautiful purple and yellow flowers with shiny black berries containing sweet inky juices. Every part of the plant is extremely poisonous, so don't touch it without gloves! The soldiers of Macbeth poisoned an army of invading Danes by giving them a belladona cocktail during a truce – the Danes drank loads of the stuff (proper pissheads the Danes), passed out, and were easily murdered in their sleep by the Scots. Serves 'em right I say, coming over here causing trouble! The juice of the

THORNAPPLE

A strange-looking plant with little spiky balls containing seeds so loaded in venom that should you drop a couple in a reservoir you could wipe out London! It is a narcotic and psychotropic herb whose poison, which can be destroyed by cooking or boiling, brings on madness, delirium, paranoia. Put it in his cup of tea, open the window and tell him Arsenal have lost. He'll be jumping out of that window like a lemming within minutes. A great little poison. Loads of fun.

So there you go – happy poisoning. And remember, there's no point doing it if you're going to get caught.

PERFORMANCE ARTIST

A term used to describe an act absolutely devoid of talent.

PAN PIPES

The music of the mountains and other such crap. Pan pipes sound to me like someone blowing into a milk bottle. Drive me insane.

PERIOD PAINS

Janet Street-Porter recommends a cheese sarnie. She reckons a mouthful of bread and fat takes your mind off the pain. Various herbal teas and Bach Flower Remedies also come highly recommended, but personally I say you can't beat taking to your bed with the leccy blanket on full and a bottle of whisky and a few Nurofen inside you. Takes your mind off anything.

PRINCIPLES

Quite honestly, it's not worth having any. Especially if you're over forty. Seize what's on offer and have no second thoughts. Life's like a jumble sale – you can root around for something special and never find it, or you can grab something that's cheap and cheerful instead. Forget your principles, nail up your conscience and get out and take what's yours.

POETRY

I love poetry: the great classics of Byron, Wordsworth and Pam Ayres. I write the odd verse myself when the urge takes me. My pal Liz Dawn went to Rome to visit the Pope, so I wrote this ode to commemorate the occasion:

Elizabeth Dawn, the star of a
*   soap,*
Was summoned to Rome by Il
*   Papa, the Pope.*
'Please tell me', he said, 'for I
*   desperately need to know,*
If they ever freed Deidre Rashid?'

(Our Vera went to Rome. I told her she must visit the Sistine Chapel and see Michaelangelo's paintings. When she came back home she said she went to the Sistine Chapel but she never saw any evidence of the great man's works – the daft cow forgot to look up – it's all on the ceiling isn't it!)

I'm staying in bed, I'm depressed.
I'm not getting washed
And I'm not getting dressed.
You heard what I said, I'm
*   depressed.*

It's this lousy weather
That makes me feel moody.
I can't even be arsed
Watching Richard and Judy.

So keep all visitors away
And unplug the phone,
'Cos as Garbo would say
*   'I vant to be alone.'*

I love eavesdropping on buses. Old women have the best conversations and when they talk about something like sex or cancer they say 'the word' in an exaggerated, barely audible voice. Thus cancer becomes 'an-ah'. I love the way their conversation flits from subject from different subjects for no real reason whatsoever.

Old Ladies on a Coach

Old age isn't fun
If you fart when you run
For the coach on a trip
To York Minster.

On a day trip you go
'Cos your spirits are low
I never married, you say,
I'm a spinster.

Not that I'm bothered,
I'm here with my friend,
She's just been made a widow.
She lives in Southend.

Remember that coach trip?
The one to Pwllheli,
The big luxury one with the
Lav and the telly?

Well there's nothing on this,
They don't even sell tea.
D'you think the driver will stop?
'Cos I must have a wee.

Do you fancy a sweet?
Are they hard? No, they're chewy.
They were dear, came from Marks,
They've been soaked in Drambuie.

Has she got false teeth?

Every one in her head!
She had a mouth full
*   of gums,*
Now she's like Mr Ed.'

They found her in bed,
Nobody could wake her,
The Ted said she's dead
You'd best call undertaker.

And we were going to go
To the Ideal Home Exhibition.
The toilets I know
Are in a beautiful condition.

Still, they're quite nice in York,
Shall I get the sandwiches out?
I could never touch pork.
D'you know our Harold's got gout?

The Miracle

On a holiday with Saga,
As you drink your Spanish lager
With a widow who's discovered
*   HRT,*

You'll find you're getting rather
*   pally,*
Later on back at her chalet,
When she lets you put your hand
upon her knee.

In the dark you take your shirt off,
She's already got her skirt off
And you're the 'only man I've slept
*   with since Stan died'.*

Get her bra off and then her girdle,
And you've reached the final
*   hurdle,*
St Viagra, how you've saved
an old man's pride!

R

To be honest if it doesn't fit on toast then I can't be bothered making it. I can cook but I wouldn't say that I particularly enjoy it. I cook out of necessity, and not for any particular pleasure – if I want that then I'll explore other avenues! Considering the amount of cookery programmes that are shown on telly I'm surprised we aren't a nation of masterchefs. I'm addicted to them, especially Delia. She makes it sound so easy and her kitchen's beautiful 'cos you know she films it in her house. She just gets up, has a wash and pops downstairs. They film her making the breakfast and she talks while she does it. I'd love to know how she finds time to look after that dirty big garden you can see outside the kitchen window. It's immaculate, unlike mine, which looks like a cemetery in a Hammer movie.

RECIPES

The kitchen is spotless, her pans gleam, her hob shines bright, she cooks, writes books, goes on the telly, and still manages to run a home with minimum fuss. She makes me bloody sick. It's not normal. I always read cookery books when I'm in bed alone. Drooling over the recipe for strawberry pavlova is a good substitute for a shag.

Nouvelle cuisine pisses me off. I want me dinner, not two peas, a carrot and the ankle from some poor unfortunate tiny lamb arranged artistically on a huge plate. One mouthful and you could demolish the lot and for this you pay a fortune.

I don't like food smothered in sauces. I don't mind if it's a fish finger covered in tomato sauce, or a cauli with a bit of cheese on top. And I could never stomach a piece of meat that was almost raw. Sometimes it's served so 'rare' that an injection from a vet would have it up on its feet and running round a field again. It's so undercooked, with a bright yellow sauce covering it entirely, the blood from the meat mixing into the sauce. Bright red against yellow, like blood in the yolk of an egg – errgh!! I like simple food. Had I lived in Victorian times and had the misfortune to be a domestic servant I would have had 'a good, plain, cook' on my cv.

Comfort food is economical and healthy, fashionable restaurants now include a number of common dishes on their menus.

Concassé de petits pois
Pommes frittes
Poulet au chateau Marie

Chicken, chips and mushy peas in other words.

Duchesse potatoes is your plain old mashed spud without its fancy hat on.

It's all the rage now – meat and two veg in the smart restaurants is considered acceptable, providing of course it costs a fortune, that makes it haute cuisine. Whatever restaurants call sausage and mash to make it appear up-market it's still a sausage with spuds, simple fayre, and its nice to see all those dishes on the menu.

Here's a selection of quick and easy recipes for you to try at home. Quick, easy, economical and full of the taste and goodness of 'Home Made Food.'

CHAMP

A great favourite in our house, it's a recipe of my mother's, a traditional Irish dish of mashed spuds and scallions.

2lb freshly cooked mashed potatoes
a good big dollop of butter
1 bunch of scallions or spring onions
drop of milk
salt and pepper

Here's what you do:
Chop the scallions, green bit as well as the white and cook in a few tablespoons of milk. Gently simmer and then drain the milk into a cup. Don't chuck it away.
Add a generous dollop of butter to the mashed spuds. Melt the rest of the butter, add the cooked scallions, beat them into the spuds and add enough milk to make them smooth and creamy. Check your seasoning. If all is to your satisfaction, transfer to a warm dish, make a well in the top of the spuds and pour more melted butter in. Sprinkle with freshly chopped parsley and chives.
Dieticians will throw their hands up in horror at the high fat content of this dish. Bugger them, it's delicious, and you might as well be hung for a sheep as a lamb. You can also use scrambled egg – with a decent dollop of double cream added to make it all the more creamy – as a filling for the well. Enjoy.

SCOUSE

A traditional Liverpool dish that's like a sort of lamb stew served with pickled cabbage. Me mouth's watering thinking about it. I make a pan of scouse now and then but I wouldn't recommend my recipe. It's not that it tastes awful, It's just there's a better one. Everyone on Merseyside has a different recipe for scouse so I rang Liverpool's most popular DJ and biggest scrubber, Peter Price, to help me try and find out. He announced it over the radio on his breakfast show which is listened to by millions of people. I believe you can even get it as far as Southport, not that that's any good – they're posh in Southport and won't eat anyting that hasn't been soaked in extra virgin olive oil and balsamic vinegar and served with a rocket salad first. Anyway, Pricey put the A.P.B. out over the airwaves and was inundated with listeners recipes for scouse. They were all carefully read and eventually the pile of recipes was whittled down to ten. I made ten pans of scouse and a select group of guests were asked to give their opinion. They were all dynamic, but this was the most popular one.

A big thanks to all you listeners of Pricey's show for taking the time to write in.

Dear Lily
My recipe for Proper Scouse is as follows.

Breast of lamb
1 1/2 lbs carrots
smallish turnip

large Spanish onions
6 King Eddy potatoes
Salt, pepper, oxo cubes

Put chopped breast of lamb in water with salt, pepper and 2 oxos.

Bring to boil, cover and simmer for about 1 hour.

Put chopped carrots, turnip and onions in pan with the meat. Cover and simmer for about 3/4 hour. Lastly, put diced King Eddys on top, put in a little more salt, pepper on potatoes, bring to boil, cover and simmer for another 3/4 hour, then stir in a figure of eight movement, mixing all the ingredients until the potatoes fall a little.

Now the secret, do not eat until the next day. The fat will have formed on top. Remove all the fat before heating up to eat. Heat properly, stirring occasionally, eat and enjoy with sweet pickled beetroot and crispy bread. Stew is made with diced beef, not scouse. If you like I'll make you a pan and pop it into the radio station.

From Mary Martin

SALADS

Salads don't have to be boring! It's easy to liven up a salad. Serve it with a kingsize bar of Cadbury's Dairy Milk Chocolate. It makes a dreary old lettuce appetising, and you'll have no trouble getting the kids to eat up!

HOW TO MAKE STOCKS

A dominatrix's dungeon is not complete without the addition of a set of wooden stocks. You can pop your customer in while he's waiting for his turn on the rack. All you need are some wooden planks, a hinge, and a padlock. Easy as pie. However, if you don't feel capable of making your own then order one from our mail order catalogue – only £179.00 (ex.-VAT). Each set of beautiful mediaeval stocks are made out of hard wearing MDF that has been painstakingly hand-painted to look like real wood. Adjustable as well, you can raise or lower our stocks to accommodate your tallest or smallest punter. Adjustable head and arm holes too. These beautiful stocks are hand-finished in simulated antique brass and come complete with a beautiful brass padlock, available in three different shades of verdigris. Hurry while stocks last! Take advantage of this special offer and buy now and we will send you a free hangman's hood, handcrafted in black chamois leather and a 300-volt cattle prod – with eezy grip rubber handle!

The other type of stock is very easy to prepare. Simply pop an old chicken carcass into a pan with some celery, carrots, turnip, onion and leek. Add a bay leaf, 10 black peppercorns, parsley and seasoning. Bring to the boil and then simmer for three quarters of an hour on a low light. Strain into a jug and reserve. Discard veg and chicken carcass.

If you can't be arsed with the mess, then try this method.

You need:
1 stock cube (beef/lamb/chicken)

Add boiling water (after you've unwrapped the stock cube and popped it into a pyrex jug)
Stir
Voila! One jug of stock.

PERFECT SCRAMBLED EGG

I can't stomach eggs. I used to quite like them until I cracked a free-range one into the frying pan and I was greeted by a half-formed chicken embryo that slid round the frying pan like that thing in Alien. I've never touched one since.
My granddaughter Kylie-Marie loves a dish of scrambled egg served with toast for her breakfast so I face up to my phobia to make it for the darling.

| 3 large eggs | Butter |
| Double cream | Salt & pepper |

Beat the eggs with a fork (break 'em first into a bowl) add salt and pepper. Melt the butter in a small pan, don't let it burn. Butter goes brown when it's burnt. Add the beaten eggs and stir with a fork – keep 'em moving. When the egg starts to congeal into a runny yellow mass, remove from the heat and add a dollop of cream. Keep stiring, the eggs will continue to cook in the heat of the pan, so there's no need to put them back on the stove. It depends on how firm or runny you like your eggs before deciding they are cooked, they should be creamy moist (ugh!) and slightly runny. Transfer onto a slice of hot buttered toast and serve. Garnish with brown sauce.

● Adults can add a drop of Tabasco to the eggs or if you're feeling in a glamorous mood how about some smoked salmon chopped into small pieces? Delicious with crispy bacon as well.

PERFECT FISH AND CHIPS

1 Lay the table. You need: place mats; knives and forks; mugs; bag of sugar; bottle of milk; salt and pepper; bottle of Sarson's Malt Vinegar; bottle of sauce, either brown or red or both; jar of pickled onions; large white sliced loaf and a packet of butter. Bottle of Irn Bru or Tizer is optional.

2 Boil a kettle and carefully fill a hot water bottle. Place this in the bottom of your shopping basket along with a jumper. Fill the kettle again but don't switch it on. Pop three tea bags in the pot and warm your plates by soaking them in a clean washing-up bowl of hot water.

3 Put your mack and headscarf on and go to the nearest fish and chip shop.

4 Queue in the chippy, passing the time by listening to some juicy gossip from the woman who works part time in the Crown and Cushion. Place order, request that they are wrapped and not open.

5 Place the parcels of fish and chips on the hot water bottle in your shopping basket and cover with the jumper. It's wise not to use one of your own jumpers as it will retain the odour of the fish and chips. I use my sister's. There's a slight whiff of vinegar about her anyway so she never notices.

6 Go home. Do not stop to chat. Do not go into the pub for a quick one.

7 Get home, take mack off. Switch kettle on and take the plates out of the bowl. Dry with a cleanish tea towel. Unwrap fish and chips and lay on plates, either with or without the paper. Open carton of peas or curry and arrange at the side of the fish.

ON THE GAME SOUP

If you're a working girl who likes something warm inside her then this is the perfect supper for you. Just the thing after a long night walking the streets or hunched up in the back of a Ford Fiesta giving relief massage for £15 to a civil servant whose wife doesn't understand him. Warming and nourishing, this soup is easy and cheap to make.

You need:
1 onion	salt and pepper
1 carrot	1 oz of plain flour
stick of celery	2 teaspoons redcurrant jelly
3oz butter	cup of red wine
2 pints of game stock (see recipe below)	4 tbs. brandy
bay leaf	4 tbsp. sherry
	drop of port

Game Stock
1 tin of venison or game soup

That's all you need, add a little water if required. You can make your own stock using the carcasses of ptarmigan, venison, quail and pheasant. It is helpful if you have a Tory MP amongst your clientele with an estate in Scotland. You can ask him to bring you some back. Failing that you can forget it. Where on earth do you buy ptarmigan and what the hell is it?

8 The kettle should be boiled, so pour the boiling water on the tea bags and cover pot.

9 Take the plates to the table, chivvy family to sit down.

10 Return to kitchen for teapot and a teaspoon, which you always forget.

11 Sit down yourself and after you've buttered bread and poured tea you can enjoy this traditional dish.

● Make chip butties if you like. To enjoy this family meal to its fullest, it helps if you read a book or paper propped up against the milk bottle. You can also watch tv. Enjoy.

To
make
the soup:
Prepare and chop
the veg. Melt butter
in a frying pan and
saute the veg (fry 'em in
other words). Add the
stock, bay leaf and salt and
pepper. Simmer gently for an
hour. While this is simmering you
can pop out and do a couple of
punters.

Wash hands and make a roux with the flour and butter. In vulgar parlance, melt butter in a pan, stir in the flour and fry til light brown.

Strain the soup and stir in the roux. Bring to the boil and cook for a further 2 minutes. Add redcurrant jelly and booze. Bring to the boil, simmer for a minute. If you are wearing a beret, striped top and fishnets, then serve with French bread. If you're dressed in a leather corset and spiked heels then a strong German pumpernickel might be more appropriate. A shell suit or anorak goes well with Mother's Pride thick-sliced white loaf.

SAFETY IN THE KITCHEN

✂ A kitchen is a dangerous place, unattended chip pains can spell disaster. If a fire breaks out in your kitchen don't hesitate to act quickly. Run upstairs and get your household insurance policy from the shoebox in the bottom of your wardrobe and evacuate the building.

✂ Ring the Fire Brigade from your neighbour's house then stand in the street in your slippers in a state of distress. Wait until a burly fireman puts his arm round you to concole you before you stop screaming.

✂ Move to temporary accommodation in a Social Services B&B while Housing find you a new house or flat. Claim on your insurance – don't forget to mention the diamond and ruby tiara, necklace with matching earrings and your library of priceless first editions in your claim. When the cheque finally arrives you can, to quote Viv Nicholson, 'Spend, spend, spend', preferably on clothes, a flash car and a holiday in the sun. Don't worry about furniture for the new flat – get a grant off the Social. Order stuff from your catalogue omitting to tell them that you've changed address. Slip your postman a couple of bob to reroute them to your new home. Apply to Access for a credit card and when it arrives get your partner or a pal to sign it in your name and then go on a glorious spending spree. Tell Access that the card never arrived – that signature isn't yours, so there's no need to worry about the handwriting experts if they call 'em in.

✂ It's easy to turn the disaster of a house fire into a triumph.

Vera
Cheeseman Sweetbreads

My sister adores offal – the way she licks into a steaming plate of tripe would gladden your heart. Pig's belly and boiled sheep's head are regular dishes served up at La Cheeseman's intimate dinner parties. You can guarantee that after a Sunday Munch of Roast Chicken you'll find Vera perched on top of the spin dryer stripping the carcass bare. The noise she makes! Her glasses and face always end up smeared with chicken fat. She loves to chew on a pig's foot until there's nothing left but couple of knucklebones bleached white and bare by her powerful sucking. She's in her element but the pig isn't too happy about it! Sweetbreads are one of her favourites. Here's her own personal recipe for sweetbreads à la Cheeseman.

You Need:

1lb calves' sweetbreads (calves' testicles are larger than lambs', so Vera informs me)
Tin of tomatoes
Cup of water

Small onion
Salt and pepper
2 dog hairs
1 human hair (long)
Tsp. cigarette ash
1/2 cup of white wine

Soak the sweetbreads for 1 hour in cold salted water, pop 'em into a pan of fresh salt water and bring to the boil. Cook for 15 minutes, drain and leave to get cold. Remove the veiny membrane and reserve.

Put sweetbreads in a greased pyrex dish and add rest of ingredients, chop the onion first. Cook in a moderate oven (gas mark 4) for 40 minutes. (Vera drinks the rest of the bottle while she's waiting for this mouth-watering dish to cook.)

Take the reserved membrane and arrange into an attractive rose shape to garnish the sweetbread and serve with sauce or salad cream.

TRANMERE TRIFLE

I've always had the reputation for serving wonderful trifles. Marco Pierre White got down on his knees and begged me for the recipe but I refused to reveal it until he bunged me a couple of quid. I've guarded this recipe jealously for years . . . until now – so here it is, the recipe for my much-applauded trifle.

Sugar
Packet of trifle sponges
Tin custard powder
2 pints of milk
Large pot of whipping cream
Jelly
1 banana
Tin of fruit cocktail

Tin of raspberries
Pot of strawberry jam
I maraschino cherry
Brandy, Bacardi, Champagne or white wine, advocaat and sherry
Roasted almonds
I Cadbury's flake
Packet of hundreds and thousands

Break the sponge fingers up and coat them with jam. Line the bottom of a big glass bowl with a layer of sponge. Add some fruit cocktail and pour on a liberal dose of sherry and brandy. Cover with more sponge, add fruit and repeat until you've used up all the sponge and fruit, layer by layer. Cover in raspberries and soak in sherry. Make sure you've used enough booze – this is not a recipe for teetotallers.

VEGETABLES

What to do with swede, sprouts and cabbage.

You need: 1 Pedal bin

Put all the above straight into the bin, there's nothing you can do with these revolting vegetables to make them edible. You could try soaking the sprouts in brandy then rolling them in melted chocolate, it disguises their gunmetal taste. But I'm afraid cabbage and swede are fit for nothing but pig swill.

REVENGE

It's true, revenge is a dish best served cold – don't attempt anything when you're in a blazing temper, you'll do something childish and petty. Wait until you've cooled down, allow your grievance to simmer and fester inside of you. Dwell on the dirty deed that has been done to you, let hatred grow in your heart like wild mint, plot your revenge with a clear calculating mind. It might take years before you see a chance to set your plan into action, but when it happens – wham! Your victim won't know what has hit them. Don't get mad, get even!

Make the jelly up using half water, half champagne or wine. Pour over the sponge and fruit and leave to set. You can add fruit to the jelly if you like but I think that there's enough vitamins in my trifle already so I leave the jelly as Chivers intended it.

Make a pint of custard as directed on the tin, pour over jelly and allow to cool and set.

Make a second pint of custard using half milk/half advocaat. Pour over the set custard and cover with sliced banana.

Whip the cream adding half a cup of Bacardi. When the cream is firm spoon over the top layer of custard, sprinkle hundreds and thousands, roasted almonds and the flake. Pop the cherry in the middle and serve.

**WARNING
DON'T DRIVE OR TRY TO OPERATE HEAVY MACHINERY IF YOU'VE HAD A BOWL OF TRANMERE TRIFLE.**

S

STRIPTEASE

The noble art of ecdysiasm is dead. The definition of striptease is the act of removing one's attire to music. These days a stripper doesn't wear any clothes to take off. As soon as they appear they're in the buff. There's no teasing involved. It's more of your 'simulated sex'. They wrap their legs round a pole and pretend to have intercourse with it! I'm proud to admit that in the early days I was a stripper, although in my day it was considered an art form. The professional stripteaser would appear on stage lit by a surprise pink and proceed to disrobe in time to the music, taking her time, teasing a glove off with her teeth, lowering a shoulder strap, 'Make 'em wait' was the key word. It would take me two days to get down to me G-string.

Every stripper had her own individual gimmick: balloons, feathers, fans, doves that undressed you, tassel twirling – you name it. There was also a set formula to a strip that most strip women, regardless of their gimmick, stuck to. At the Blue Balloon, the various steps were known in succession as:

1 **THE FLASH OR THE ENTRANCE.**

2 **THE PARADE. The stripper would literally parade slowly around the stage,**

allowing the audience to get a good look at her while she took a good look at them.

3   **THE GRIND. Writing the letter 'O' with your pelvic girdle, very slowly – this was followed by the 'bump'.**

4   **THE BUMP. Moving the hips forward with a snap accentuated by a thump on a kettle drum.**

5   **THE TEASE. The first item of clothing to go are the gloves. Thrown, not into the audience like they do in old movies, but into the wings. Strippers aren't made of money you know. Opera length evening gloves are hard to find if you should lose one. You try finding peach satin evening gloves on a Saturday morning in Mansfield Market.**

6   **THE FULL WORKS. A glove off, the audience are eager for more. They show their appreciation by whooping, whistling and cheering. The stripper will parade with an insolent smirk on her face, like a boxer pacing the ring after winning the first round. She may murmur under her breath 'Take it easy boys, take it easy', or some other cliché. The other glove will be removed, and then slowly, one at a time she will drop her shoulder straps, turning her back to the crowd. She brings her arm up elegantly behind her and before she pulls the zipper down (made easy with the use of a long black hairpin attached to the top of the zipper) she will look over her shoulder with a wry smile and raised eyebrows.**

The Queen of the Striptease was without doubt the incomparable Gypsy Rose Lee. She had brains as well as beauty and elevated striptease with an act that was witty and elegant. The darling of the literary set, she had friends in high places. She was no stranger to the criminal fraternity. At one time she was the Moll of the notorious gangster, 'Waxy' Gordon. A woman of originality, strength and great courage – the musical version of her life, Gypsy, didn't do her justice. They don't make 'em like her anymore.

Across the pond we had our very own Gypsy in the form of Phyllis Dixey – the girl the Lord Chamberlain banned! Miss Dixey performed at the Whitehall Theatre for the duration of the war and despite a rather prim school marmish approach to strippin' she was a huge star. There was also Jane from the Daily Mirror, Carla the Tassel Twirler, Bonnie Belle the Ding Dong Girl, Alky Selter, Bumps and Burps, Gaby Rose Lynn – the roll call is endless.

Some stripteasers preferred to be called an exotic dancer, which meant that they left their drawers on.

I remember the first show I was in for Paul Raymond. On the marquee in front of the theatre it said in huge letters 'Lily Savage in Call Her Harlot' – it should've said 'Charlotte' but a few letters fell off.

Our Vera was a cooch dancer for a while. She used to pick a hanky up by her teeth. One night she lost the hanky and had to use a blanket. The weight of it pulled her dentures out of her mouth. A wit in the audience shouted 'Take 'em off! Not take 'em out!'

'STREETS OF LONDON'

I hate this song. Usually you hear it played by buskers outside Tube stations or hippies at folk clubs. Even modern priests sing it at mass.

Kick the lot of them in the gob.

STREET ENTERTAINERS

These really piss me off. I hate mime artists and those stupid sods who pretend to be robots and make silly jerky movements right in your face. Poke 'em in the eye and say 'Get a fuckin' job!' The same goes for stilt-walkers, jugglers, fire eaters and gobshite escapologists who make you test their chains to prove they're real.

These sad bastards can't get a booking in a club, or even at a benefit, so undeterred they inflict it on to us in the street, the unsuspecting public. When I'm out shopping I like to be able to make a quick exit out of a shop and don't want my exit blocked because some hippy on stilts is juggling on the bloody pavement.

Street entertainers, I hate you, keep away.

STAINS

As a mother and homemaker there isn't a stain invented I can't tackle. Modern detergents and stain removers won't remove a difficult stain and dry-cleaners these days are crap.

So what do you do if you spill red wine down your blouse? Get tar on your bathing suit? Or find your ferret has done its business on your best slacks?

CHIP FAT

If you learned how to lower your chip basket gently into the hot fat then you wouldn't get splattered. But if it does happen, cover the stain with fuller's earth and leave for twenty-four hours. Cat litter works just as well. Make sure the cat hasn't used it first.

BLUE INK

Milk – preferably red hot or as sour as Princess Margaret – is the answer. Rub it in and rinse off, or soak the garment in it. If the stain is on the carpet sprinkle it with salt first. Hoover up, then apply the milk. Shampoo afterwards or the place will stink.

RED INK

A swine to shift. You should first dab on some ammonia and then sponge it out. If this doesn't work, then try meths.

RED WINE

If the waiter knocks a carafe of house red all over you, then don't go screaming like a banshee. Remain calm and ask to see the manager. Tell him you require a bottle of their best white wine – on the house – and it has to be a good wine else it won't work. Mop up the excess red wine with a napkin and then, with a clean napkin underneath the stain, pour on just enough white wine to soak it. Leave it while you polish off the rest of the bottle, then go to the lav and rinse the stain out with lukewarm water. And it's gone. This is also effective on carpets.

BEETROOT

Our Vera's forever pickling beetroot in the bathroom sink. Consequently I'm always finding pink stains on my beautiful towels. This method always shifts any stains. Wipe the stain with a damp bar of soap and then moisten with either vodka or gin. Rub gently, then rinse under running water. Resist the temptation to drink the booze.

BLOOD

If members of your family come home on a Saturday night like mine, splattered in blood after another fight outside the chippy, then this tip will be invaluable. If the blood is wet, then the immediate application of cold salty water will shift it. Dried bloodstains are a bugger to move. Try the cold salty water routine, and then apply a drop of household ammonia. Wash in cold water until the stain disappears. Alternatively you could try dyeing the garment bright red.

GRASS STAINS

It's all very well having a bit of slap and tickle in the park, but grass stains on the back of your skirt or on the knees of your white slacks need careful handling. A moist bar of soap rubbed over the area is very effective. Stubborn grass stains can be shifted with a drop of glycerine or meths without harming the fabric.

To avoid further grass stains take your clothes off before having sex outdoors or do it in a bed or the back of a car, avoiding grassy knolls.

HAIR LACQUER

This can do terrible damage to some fabrics, satin in particular. It's always better to do your hair before you get dressed. However, if lacquer has stained your favourite blouse, then soak it in a bowl of cold water with a generous measure of Borax.

LIPSTICK

If it's lippy on your clothes, then dab on some oil of eucalyptus, leave it to soak in and then wash with soap and water. If, however, it's some other whore's lippy on his clothes, then this isn't the time to talk about stain removal. Punch his face in and get a divorce.

VASELINE

Got a little smear of Vaseline on your duvet cover or bed linen? Don't despair. Just remember Vaseline will set forever if it comes into contact with hot water. Tamp with a few drops of turps before washing.

SEMEN

Some men aren't fussy where they wipe their appendage – on the hem of your nightie, on your beautiful Egyptian cotton bed linen, even on your curtains! Although it looks like a hard stain to remove, it is in fact easily shifted in a normal wash. Insist your gentlemen callers use a towel!

SWEAT

Depends on your sweat type, which can be either acid or alkali, depending on your state of health. An acid sweat is shifted with ammonia, and alkali comes out with lemon juice. You'll have to experiment to see what kind of sweater you are.

DOG PISS

If the dog pees on the carpet on no account rub his nose in it. Boot the dog out into the back yard, then splash on some soda water, mop up and repeat. If you do this immediately then the pee won't stain. House your dog in a kennel.

URINE

If your old man comes home pissed and misses the bowl when he's taking a leak and soaks your beautiful pink bathroom carpet – rub his nose in it, boot him out into the back yard and get the soda water out. Finish off with a drop of Dettol.

CAT PEE

If your cat pees behind the telly then use the soda water treatment as well. Don't use your best scent to hide the smell. It's a waste of good scent and will stain the carpet. Rub in a few drops of ammonia to disguise the odour and boot the cat into back yard. Discourage cat from returning.

STRETCH LIMOUSINES

You should only travel in a white stretch limousine if you are:

✔ **An up-and-coming trainee boy band**

✔ **A very minor celebrity**

✔ **A northern club owner arriving at the opening of his new club with a soap star**

✔ **A group of girls or lads from Romford going 'up West' for a flash night out**

✔ **A desperate sad bastard who wants to appear important**

✔ **A footballer's ex-wife**

SEX AND VIOLENCE ON TELEVISION

There's a lot of it isn't there? So please don't think me a prude when I say that sex and violence on television should be gratuitous. I'm with Mary Whitehouse on that one.

SWEDEN

Just as cold and depressing as Finland only with stricter licensing laws. The men are all called Benni and the women Frieda and because it's like prohibition over there, the Swedes get very excited when they have a drink. They make a show of themselves in public by knocking pints of lager back in one, farting and fighting – which explains Ulrika Jonsson.

SISTER

What is a sister? A bloody nuisance at times I know but I wouldn't swap mine for a monkey up a stick.

Better the devil you know … I've got a plate hanging on the kitchen wall that our Vera brought me back from her holiday in Blackpool. It's called 'Sister' and it's a poignant piece of prose that personally I find very moving and I think it sums up the kind of relationship that sisters have.

Sister

Remember the old days?
Times were hard, we were poor
You'd share my last fag
And I'd share your cold sore.

We'd share the same razor
To shave our armpits
We shared the same comb
Even shared the same nits.

She may never show it
But she cares underneath
She'd lend her last penny
Even lend you her teeth.

And at the end of the road
When we're too old to roam
We'll share a commode
In an old people's home.

It's a beautiful verse isn't it? And if you are lucky enough to have a sister then you'll understand what it means. I wish I knew who the author of this lovely poem was.

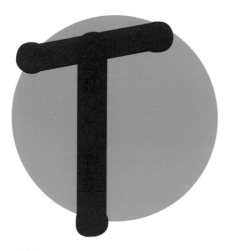

THAILAND

I love the Far East, after all I spent some time there, but I hate Thailand. Bangkok is the dirtiest, smelliest, pushiest hellhole that I ever set foot in and I've been to some places in my time. The brochures enthuse about Bangkok's 'naughty nightlife', a euphemism for the exploitation of child prostitutes. Bangkok is hustle city – a white woman travelling alone can't walk the streets in peace without some scrawny pimp offering you sex with everything from his granny to his parrot.

They have some pretty disturbing 'shows' as well – 'LIVE ANIMAL SHOWS'. A tout outside a club called 'The Barnyard' asked me if I'd like to step inside and 'see a show man with a duck'. I knew damn well it wasn't going to be Keith Harris and Orville, so I declined.

One nightclub I popped into had a young lady who did a speciality act with ping-pong balls. If you've seen that movie Priscilla Queen of the Desert then you'll know what I'm on about. She sat on a stool in the middle of the stage, a big smile on her face, her legs wide open and fired ping-pong balls from her muff across the room. I wasn't impressed – there used to be a stripper in the Blue Balloon Club who did the same act only using rugby balls. The crowd would go wild! It was a bugger if you had to follow her. The National Lottery should get hold of the ping pong girl, that would be a novel way of picking the balls and a lot more interesting than the machine they use now – might improve their viewing figures as well.

TILLER GIRLS

I am proud to say that I am an honorary Tiller Girl. I have thrown me legs up with the original 1960s Tiller Girls on numerous occasions. The Tillers are a fine bunch of women, who, despite the fact that they will never see 40 again have the stamina and energy of dancers half their age. How do they do it? What is the secret of maintaining a youthful and glamorous appearance? How does a

cut the mustard when you hit your fifties. They dance just as brilliantly as they did 30 years ago. The line-up is still a disciplined precision machine, all the girls moving as one. The occasional HRT patch might fly off a thigh and whizz over the audience's heads like a discus, and now and then one of the older girls might break wind during a particularly energetic routine. But it's always a silent one – these women are pros!

woman of 74 get her legs in the air? Their secret is simple: booze, slimming tablets, HRT patches and lots of sex. Every Tiller has at least four patches stuck on her back and a Tiller line-up contains more hormones than an East German athlete's urine specimen.

They can go out all night partying until the dawn breaks. You often see the odd Tiller wandering across Trafalgar Square, the feathers in her head-dress slightly askew after a night's raving at Trade.

The Tillers are living proof that you can still

Being a member of the exclusive Tiller Girls was very prestigious. Discipline was tough, the girls were drilled like army privates by a toughie named Miss Barbara. She ruled them with a rod of iron, anyone stepped out and it was 'bye-bye'. Tillers were expected to have high standards, only the best would do, especially if you were a London Palladium Tiller. Betty Boothroyd was only a Tiller for a very short time and that was as a member of a small group recruited for provincial panto. So she wasn't really a proper Tiller.

Back in the 1960s becoming a Palladium Tiller girl was a highly prestigious and much sought-after job. Only the crème de la crème of dancers made the grade. As well as being able to dance, a Tiller was required to be tall, slim, beautiful and elegant and conduct herself like 'a lady' at all times. When I look at the 1960s' Tillers today, I don't know how half of them got round the conduct clause, especially Rose – a former Lido lovely at the Floral Pavilion, New Brighton, before she became one of the jewels in the Tiller crown. It is heavily rumoured that Rose once had an amorous encounter with Tom Jones in the prop room of the Palladium. I'm not definite it was Tom – it could have been Jimmy Clitheroe. I only caught a bit of the conversation that fellow Tillers Kath and June were having because Kath was whispering and I was two seats in front of them on the bus. I know she had a torrid affair with Arthur Askey because a pal of mine Gina, an exiled Russian Princess who had been forced to take a position as a dancer in Fiddler on the Roof, told me so. Arthur stepped in after Topol fell off it (the roof, that is) one night, breaking his arm which meant of course he couldn't fiddle and had to leave the show. Arthur was a marvellous fiddler and as nimble as a marmoset monkey. Gina said he used to leap off the water butt during the 'If I were a rich man' number as if he had wings.

She remembers Rose visiting Arthur's dressing room after a Wednesday matinee and by the time it came to do the evening performance poor Arthur was hardly able to stand. He was so exhausted after a session with our Rose that the understudy had to go on. She had a very healthy appetite when it came to l'amour did Rose and tiny Arthur couldn't keep up with her insatiable demands.

Big-hearted Arthur's opening line was his famous catchphrase – a cheery 'Hello playmates', to which the audience would respond with an even cheerier 'Fuck off'. Some nights he would forget it because he was so exhausted and Gina would have to prompt him. He used to forget whole chunks of 'The Bee Song' which had been put in to replace the dreary 'Match maker, match maker' number. Gina, dressed as a Jewish daisy, would squirm with embarrassment as a confused Arthur flew around her flapping his wings desperately trying to remember what came after,

'Buzz, buzz, buzz, buzz,
Honey Bee, Honey Bee. . . .'

However I'm digressing – this is supposed to be about the Tiller Girls not Arthur Askey. To be a proper Tiller you need to have danced in the kickline on a Sunday Night at the London Palladium and travelled on the revolve at the end of the show to the famous la la la la la la la la laa laa music. I think it's called 'Startime' – if I'm wrong please don't write to me to put me in the clear, its not something that keeps me from my sleep.

Going round on the revolve on a Sunday Night at the London Palladium with 24 Tiller Girls and the orchestra playing the la la theme has got to be one of the greatest experiences of my life – I was high as a kite for days. (Rose had made me take a mouthful of Tenuate Dospan, a powerful slimming tablet – I was actually stuck to the ceiling.) The NHS should treat people suffering from severe depression by giving them a spin on the Palladium revolve, they wouldn't need Prozac. It's probably one of the reasons why the Tillers are so full of joie de vivre.

TRUST

D^{on't.}

TEA

The national drink. A panacea. In times of trouble and strife the cry goes up 'I'll put the kettle on and make a nice cup of tea.' It's like a safety blanket and has a calming, soothing effect on the distressed. Thank Christ for tea.

I can't face the day until I drink at least a gallon of the stuff. Dieticians and doctors say that it's bad for you. What would they rather we supped then? A bottle of vodka? I even like some of these herbal infusions – chamomile tea is reputed to induce sleep but I'm afraid it has no effect on me – I need a horse tranquilliser and a tap over the head with a mallet to get me off.

But three cheers for the amber nectar. No, not lager, but tea.

How to make the Perfect Cup of Tea

1 Put the kettle on and pop a tea bag of your favourite tea in a mug.

2 When the water has boiled pour over the tea bag.

3 Stir and leave to stew for at least three minutes. Or according to taste.

4 Remove tea bag and add milk and sugar.

5 Stir well. Enjoy with a fag and a magazine.

TRAINS

I used to really look forward to a long train journey. It was an expedition, sat in a comfortable seat, a can of lager in one hand, and a Woman's Own in the other, lazily watching the countryside race by. If I was in the mood I'd have a chat with a fellow passenger, or enjoy a little snooze, arriving at my destination refreshed and on time.

I realise now that these are the nostalgic recollections of a romantic fool and bear no resemblance to the living nightmare that rail travel is today.

Last Christmas I took the train from Euston to Liverpool Lime Street, a journey that normally takes two and three quarter hours max. Thanks to the super efficiency of Virgin Rail it took nine hours. I also had to take out a second mortgage to buy the bloody ticket. The train was jam-packed – it could've been part of a student prank for rag week: 'How many poor bastards with tons of luggage and Christmas presents can you cram on a train?'

There were no buffet facilities, but then that's no great loss considering the overpriced muck that is on offer, and the heating was turned up to maximum. Passengers standing in the aisles were wilting and fainting in the stifling atmosphere like the Calcutta Express. This was hell on wheels.

Eventually after seven hours of this torture the train came to a grinding halt at Stafford and we were flung off with the obligatory 'This train will terminate at Stafford due to a points failure. We apologise for any inconvenience.'

Never mind the apologies – give us a refund. We were transferred to an already half-full local train. A farting, little chug-chug that stopped at every single piddling station in the North West, eventually arriving at Lime Street one and a half hours later.

I stood in a mile long queue for taxis, demented, frustrated and exhausted, planning over and over in my head the hate mail I was going to send Richard Branson:

'Dear Gobshite,

Instead of friggin around in balloons, why don't you get your trains in order?

Yours,

    L. Savage.'

'Dear Gormless Bearded Twat,
    I intend to kill you and every member of your stinking family for the nightmare ordeal I've just been through…."

Childish but very satisfying. One thing was clear, I was never setting foot on a train again.

I wish I could make a decision and stick to it because at the moment I'm writing this entry in my diary from 'somewhere just outside Macclesfield', stranded again, this time on the London to Manchester train. It's taken us four hours just to get this far. I'm fit to kill. I think I'll take it out on the kid who keeps pulling faces at me over the seat in front. I'll put me fag out on his forehead, that should wipe the smile off the little get's face.

I can only assume that there is a coffin on board this train and the reason we are travelling at one mile per hour is out of respect for the deceased.

We've just crept very, very slowly into

Macclesfield Station. The Senior Conductor is announcing it over the tannoy as if we've reached the summit of Everest.

'Laydeez 'n' g'nlm'n. This is Macclesfield! Change here for …"

Fuck off.

Y'know there are certain parts of our fair country that depress the arse off me and I think Macclesfield Station is one of them. I recall an old pal of mine, an exiled Russian princess, Her Imperial Highness Regina Fong – Geena to her mates – declaring rather grandly at a small informal finger buffet to raise funds for 'Calves in Distress' (the animal not the muscle) that the faded old tea gown she was wearing was made out of 'the finest Macclesfield silk'. Personally, I thought it looked like 80% Rayon and 20% Viscose but as I had a mouthful of salmon sarnie I declined to comment.

The way your mind wanders when you're stuck on a train, after the initial outburst of temper, you eventually calm down and resign yourself to the fact that you ain't going anywhere. At the moment I'm sitting like a zombie chewing on my ticket, gazing out of the window at the delights of Macclesfield Station and I can see no evidence of the exotic silk trade. The only whiff of the Orient you'll find round here is from the Chinese take-away opposite the station. A lone trainspotter is standing next to a poster encouraging us to take advantage of a weekend break in York. Now I've never been to Macclesfield so I've no idea what it's like – it might be very nice for all I know, but at the moment I'd take advantage of a weekend break in Bosnia, anything to get out of this dump….

Suddenly a train crawls into the opposite platform, and the trainspotter suddenly becomes animated, he's so excited he's probably got a hard on. He's jumping up and down like Rumplestiltskin, making the toggles on his anorak hood bang against his glasses. This is obviously a train he hasn't spotted before so it's a big day for him. I'm sorry, but I don't get trainspotters, and I'm quite hoping that the vicious looking squaddie glaring balefully at him will get up off the bench and push him under the wheels of the next friggin' diesel, thus ending his empty and pointless existence. This might sound harsh, dear reader, but try as I might I can't see any pleasure in standing on freezing platforms (I don't mean footwear) writing down the numbers on the sides of trains. Why? What for?

A woman has just got on and has parked her carcass opposite me, and horror of horrors she's trying to strike up a conversation. I ain't talking to no one. Surely to Christ she can tell by my body language that I'm not up for 'general and polite chit chat.' I'm sat like a coiled spring, arms folded, nose pressed firmly against the window pretending to be desperately interested in Platform Two. I'm almost side on to her for God's sake, what else do I have to do to let the daft cow know that 'I vant to be alone'. I'm feeling as sociable as a pitbull with a broken bottle up its arse.

Unfortunately I'm a captive audience and she knows it. She can ramble on to her heart's content, and she is, incessantly about her sister's hysterectomy.

'I've just been to visit her', she's saying. 'She's just come out of hospital, she had fibroids like Brussels sprouts', and she demonstrates the size of these whoppers with her thumb and forefinger. 'Massive, the doctor said he's never seen anything like them. She kept them, got them in a Maxwell House jar by the side of her bed. D'you want a Liquorice Allsort?'

I refuse politely, I don't like the look of them, the paper bag is filthy.

'On a diet then?' she says. 'My poor sister was on a diet, but she don't need to now, she's lost a stone in that hospital.' Warming to her theme she leans conspiratorially across the table and lowers her voice.

'Her womb was tilted you know', she says, almost whispering. 'She couldn't wear high heels, had to go to her daughter's wedding in slippers. Crying shame, she's not the same person since they took it all away.' Her voice gets even lower, she's barely audible and I have to strain to hear her, not that I'm interested, I'm just being polite. 'She had to be cut, she needed 30 stitches in her V.A.G.I.N.A. It looked like a zip in a sports bag by the time they finished with her. Put her right off the other. Are you sure you don't want a sweet?'

I make my excuses and escape to the lav before I throw up. I'm sat on the pan smoking a fag, ignoring the 'No smoking' sign and the threat of a £500 fine. I refuse to sit in the smoking compartment, the ventilation is non-existent. Just walking through the smoking section makes your clothes and hair stink like a pub ashtray. You need a gas mask to sit in there and I'm a smoker.

Outside the door I can hear the Senior Conductor's voice on the tannoy apologising yet again for the delay and pointing out that we are in Macclesfield. No need to rub it in. This conductor is one of the microphone-happy ones. He's never off it every chance he gets he gives us a totally irrelevant bulletin. The management have obviously sent him on a training course for passenger relations and by Christ he demonstrates his newly acquired skills every three minutes, like an Asian Gladys Pugh, jollying the campers along.

The guy who runs the buffet comes on the mike next:

'Good evening ladies and gentlemen, this is your team leader speaking. The buffet car is open for tea, coffee, hot chocolate, sweet and savoury snacks, sandwiches, and a fully licensed bar.' He tells us where the buffet car is situated 'In the centre of the train in coach G' and informs us that in the event of a passenger not wishing to leave their seat a trolley service is provided and will be coming round with a selection of tea, coffee, hot chocolate . . . I feel like screaming. How many gourmet commuters will be stampeding to the buffet, desperate to sample the savoury delights of a hot bacon roll, I wonder? They look like a road accident and taste like a piece of damp cardboard warmed by the business that the dog has done on it. I go back to my seat. Mrs Womb is tucking into a 'Coronation Chicken' sandwich. Who's Coronation? Boadicea?

I get a cup of tea from the trolley service. I notice the ubiquitous Gary Rhodes has got his name plastered all over the packet of sugar.

'Smile, it's Tate and Lyle', and a facsimile of his signature 'Gary Rhodes'. Give me strength. Why would anyone want to smile at a packet of sugar? Or Gary Rhodes for that matter? On second thoughts, Gary Rhodes nailed to a door with his face smeared in dog excrement might raise a titter.

If I don't get off this train I'm going to go beserk. Just as I'm about to rip me blouse off and lie in the aisle, Gladys gets back on the mike to apologise for the delay and to let us know that we shall shortly be leaving Macclesfield. . . . Yeah! 'Course we will! The staff on trains are always really pleasant and yet these are the poor buggers we take it out on when the railway company fails to deliver the goods. It's not Andy the team leader's fault that the abortion that calls itself a spicey bean burger costs £2.49, nor is it the senior conductor's fault that the journey to Manchester takes six hours.

Have you noticed the new jargon on trains? Passengers are called 'customers', carriages are referred to as accommodation and the chief steward is now a 'team leader'. What bright spark thought this lot up?

Just as I'm about to top myself the train lurches forward and we're moving! Mrs Womb, who is just about to take a sip of scalding hot tea from its beige plastic cup spills it down her front and screams. Happy ending anyway.

Let the train take the strain? Bollocks! Jason! Get the car out!

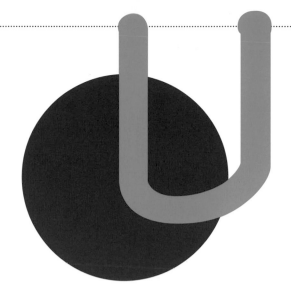

ULRIKA

If you're going to act like a man, or how you think a man acts, then why not act like a nice one? Let Richard Whiteley be your role model instead of some Millwall-supporting, pit-bull breeding, flag-waving, wife-beating arsehole.

V

VOMITING

We are talking drink-related vomiting here. I hate even having to mention vomit but, if you're going out on the piss, there is a good chance that you may bring it up again. Avoid the following drinks: Bloody Mary, Vodka and Cranberry juice, Pernod and black and Guinness. If you bring any of these back up then you will probably think, in your drunken state, that you have haemorrhaged and there is a danger that you may end up ranting and raving in your local casualty.

Vomiting in public has got to be one of the most humiliating experiences ever. But when you've got to gip, you've got to gip. Our Vera has it down to a fine art. She can be having an animated conversation at a party, and chunder mid-sentence. Cool as ice she'll just wipe the back of her hand across her gob, have a swig of her drink and carry on as if nothing has happened. Pure class.

So, if you do feel the need to vomit in public, then why not try some of the Vera Cheeseman techniques:

ON THE DANCE FLOOR

Try to avoid fellow dancers as this causes a fuss, but, with any luck, most of the writhing bodies around you will be high on hallucinogenic drugs and other cheap stimulants they bought from a friend of the bouncer, so they probably won't notice. Even if they do, they will just assume that it is another colourful hallucination. However, if you're part of a formation dance team being filmed at the Tower Ballroom in Blackpool for Come Dancing and you do one down the back of your partner's tux, you could find yourself in a tricky situation. Wave the masses of net and tulle that make up the underskirt of your frock in the air to distract attention. Try to keep your partner's back away from the camera by steering him in the other direction. Don't stop, for God's sake – carry on – you're a pro.

SEATED AT A TABLE IN A NIGHTCLUB OR A RESTAURANT

An easy one this – just pop your head under the table, throw up, and then reappear moments later saying, 'My ankle bracelet fell off. I really need to have that catch repaired. Shall we go?'

You can then exit and no one is any the wiser.

IN A TAXI

Get your head out of that window pronto! For God's sake make sure you are facing the right way, don't make the mistake of having the wind in your face. If you do let one go in the back of the cab you will have to listen to the driver's moans and will also have to pay about thirty quid so he can get the cab cleaned. A bit steep for a bit of sick if you ask me.

ON A NIGHT BUS

Isn't that what they're for?

VERA

Veronica Alice Blanche Cheeseman – the wind beneath my wings. My loyal and devoted sister. She isn't my blood sister but we are as close as if we came from the same egg. Our Vera is actually older than me by two years. Everybody assumes that I am the elder because of my protective attitude towards her and not because she looks younger. Our Vera could be any age from six to sixty!

When Vera was born, the midwife crossed herself. Little Vera wasn't like other babies, there was something very different about her that set her apart from normal children. Little Vera was born wearing a pair of perfectly formed wire NHS spectacles.

Vera's mother, Agnes Cheeseman, a young foolish slattern from the slums of Liverpool wanted nothing to do with her tiny daughter. Her first words on seeing the child were 'Get that freak away from me!'.

Vera was the result of a liaison with a hawker who worked at a travelling fairground; an unexpected, unloved and unwanted child. Her father would accept no responsibility and her mother, completely lacking in any maternal love, was only concerned about how she was going to dump the baby.

The problem was taken off her hands by Ma Witherspoon, Vera's grandmother and the terrifying matriarch of the travelling fairground. She had visited young Aggie not as a caring mother-in-law but to tell her to keep away from her son. Her precious only son was the sole heir to Ma's fortune. The fair would be passed to him when she died, and no cheap little slut like Aggie was getting her thieving hands on it while she still had breath in her body.

She bent over baby Vera's cradle to take a look at 'the Bastard' as she cruelly called our

Vera. Her beady eyes lit up when she saw the cruel trick mother nature had played on the child. This strange little thing could make a fortune if it were to be displayed in the freak show. Ma Witherspoon tapped Vera's spectacles with a jewelled claw and cackled.

'I'll do you a favour me girl, I'll take the child off your hands for ye. Here's twenty quid. As soon as your stitches are out, buy yourself a train ticket and piss off.'

And so little Vera's formative years were spent as Vera the Human Bush Baby, an exhibit in the Witherspoon Freak Show. Perched on a branch in a glass tank she was seen by thousands of people. I'm about to blow the lid on another popular myth. I was never the child star of the family, Vera was, until my mother rescued her. My Mum had retired from the ring but she occasionally liked to go and watch her old tag partner 'The Blundellsands Bomb'.

B.B. was fighting at a bank holiday fair, the Witherspoon Fair. When my Mam saw poor little Vera chewing on a stick of sugar cane in that glass tank she went ballistic. Outraged at the cruelty of displaying this child she smashed the glass with one punch and rescued Vera. She ran with the child in her arms through the back streets of Birkenhead, the Witherspoon clan in hot pursuit. She tossed Vera over the fence of the local allotments. Granny Von had a small patch she grew cabbages and marijuana plants on. Little Vera flew over the fence and landed safely in a warm mound of manure, gently rolling down the side of the steaming heap and under the leaf of one of Granny Von's prize cabbages. So when we say that our Vera was found under a cabbage patch, it's true!

Anyway, me mother took Vera in and brought Vera up as her own. I had to share a bed with her which I hated! Especially when she wet it. My mother used to say 'Which end

of the bed do you want?' and I'd reply 'The shallow end'.

When Vera was 21, she met a man (I use the term loosely) called Arthur Crawley. Both my mother and me hated 'creepy' on sight. He was a big, oily fruit who lived with his Mum, an old bitch, that we would sometimes see being pushed around in a wheelchair by Arthur on a Saturday morning in Birkenhead market. Arthur was a tight fisted, petty minded arrogant little fart who somehow managed to woo my poor sister with his silver tongue. Our Vera was just an innocent, naive and trusting young girl and she deserved better than Arthur friggin' Crawley.

She married him and started her married life in his mother's house. Arthur didn't want a bride, he wanted a slave to wait on his mother hand and foot. Vera behaved like a dutiful wife and ran around after old Mrs Crawley 24 hours a day. She cooked, cleaned, shopped and was treated like a dog. Eventually after she could stand it no longer, my Mam went round, battered poor Arthur, and brought poor Vera home, a shadow of her former self.

After she got over the Arthur business, she went to Greece for a little holiday and met a waiter called Stelious, who, surprise surprise, turned out to be another grade A c.... He came back to England with Vera (now a divorcee) and they made plans to marry. Vera was blissfully happy, she looked radiant on her wedding day, dressed in an eau de nil shift dress with a matching hat. Stelious was handsome, young, virile – he could have any woman he wanted – so why pick our Vera? As you can imagine we were very suspicious and we had every right to be.

A small reception was held in the function room of the 'Tranmere Castle' and the honeymoon was spent in Vera's room at me mother's house. That night the truth came out

SUNDAY Midden

September 20, 1998 60p www.sundaymidden.co.uk

DOG ADDICTED TO 0898 NUMBERS

THE TRUTH BEHIND LILY'S TRAGIC SISTER

Millionairess Star lives in lap of luxury while Sister lives in council house

'By the time I've bought my drugs & booze, I can't afford to feed the cats' cried Vera.

Veronica Cheeseman, sister of multimillionaire international superstar Lily Savage, has spoken for the first time about her tragic life of poverty.

STAINED

'I can't take it any more,' she told the Sunday Midden. 'Lily lives the life of Riley, swanning around the South of France with the jet set, while I scrimp and save just to have 50p to put in the meter.' At this point, Ms Cheeseman collapses,

Due to the litigious nature of Vera Cheeseman it has not been possible for the publisher to reproduce her photograph here.

sobbing into a stained hanky.

GUCCI

'Last week I asked to borrow a fiver and she just looked at me ... so I took it from her Gucci handbag when she wasn't looking. Serves her right.'

NO COMMENT

Lily Savage, thought to be holidaying incognito in Cannes, was not available for comment at the time of going to press.

PICTURE REPORTS ON PAGES 3,4,5,8,9,16&17

She'll kill me if she finds out that I've told you this tale. We refer to it, if ever, as 'The Great Tragedy'. Our Vera was never the same after it but then I'm not surprised. I'd be the same if I'd been humiliated and used like she was.

Vera's great loves these days are Bingo, booze, puzzle books, her health and scratch cards. She's also animal mad, forever bringing home injured animals that she nurses back to health. I found a hedgehog in a shoe box inside the airing cupboard once. She'd found the poor little creature in the road and brought it home.

about the marriage. Stelious cared nothing for Vera. All he wanted was a girl stupid enough to marry him and provide him with British citizenship.

Vera had got a beautiful 42-piece dinner service off the Embassy coupons. She'd smoked like a chimney to get enough coupons and kept it under her bed to be used when she married. To the tune of 'Zorba the Greek' on the gramophone a drunken Stelious smashed every piece of her beloved dinner service, packed his bags and left. She never saw nor heard of him again.

She stayed in her bedroom, sat amongst the broken remains of the dinner service in her eau de nil wedding dress for three weeks. Stelious had broken her heart along with the china.

The thing is, she was pissed and didn't see that the hedgehog had a tyre mark running along its flattened belly. The thing was dead and it was in my airing cupboard for a week stinking the place out. I had to buy new sheets. But that's our Vera, one in a million or was it won in a raffle? Whatever it was, she's my skin and blister.

WITCH

I'VE GOT THREE great aunties, Aunty Cattermole, Aunty Hecate and Aunty Venefica – known as Moll, Kate and Binnie respectively. They live together in a large detached house in Birkenhead. It's detached because the other houses in the street have been demolished but they refused to move, so the planners are going to build a Tesco Metro around it (apparently their front door will open out onto the dairy produce section when it's built).

The Savage sisters have been a familiar sight in Birkenhead for years. The villagers are slightly wary of them and cross the street when they see the formidable trio approaching, for they were rumoured to be witches. If Tranmere Rovers lose, if a frost kills early flowers or if your daughter starts spewing pea soup and spinning her head around, then the Savage sisters get the blame. This doesn't stop the superstitious villagers turning to the aunties for help, though.

Every night at dusk, you'll find young women, heavy with troubles, in the aunties' parlour seeking their help and advice and, for a small fee, those girls will be sent on their way a lot lighter. Love spells, fertility potions, even curses can be bought from my aunties for a small token.

The eldest Hecate, or Kate, is tall and willowy with long white hair that has never been cut in its life. It reaches the floor. I've never seen hair like it. She carries a walking stick that has a snake coiled round it which she calls her 'wand'. Moll is the second oldest and is never without her pet raven Mephy on her shoulder. The youngest, Binnie, has red curly hair and wears an eye patch, a habit she adopted when she spent some time in the Far East on a Chinese trading vessel in the South China Seas. She's a bit raucous and enjoys her bevvy, so we have to keep an eye on her. When I was born, the aunties came round to the house to inspect me. They wanted to see if I had any special marks on me that might signify that I had inherited their special powers. On my behind

CRAFT

was a tiny blemish (I've had it lasered since), a perfectly formed double B. It was Kate who discovered it.

'Look, my sisters,' she exclaimed, beckoning Binnie and Moll over to my cradle. 'The child has a mark.'

The aunts gathered round the cradle and took it in turns to peer at my birthmark through a magnifying glass.

'I don't believe it,' said Binnie. 'BB. What can it mean?'

'A curse?' asked Moll. 'A prophetic warning? An omen? What does it signify?'

They started to babble excitedly, offering suggestions as to what the initials BB stamped on my tiny hoop could mean. 'Brass Band!' suggested Moll. 'Or Back Bencher – maybe she'll go into politics and become prime minister!'

'She'd be better employed blowing a trumpet than hot air in the Houses of Parliament. Politicians should be out on the street with the people, making themselves known and heard by the workers not pontificating to a bunch of deadheads,' roared Binnie, who secretly bought the Socialist Worker from a woman outside the station. 'Bumble Bee, Bubble Bath, Brandy Butter, Boys Brigade . . . ' Moll chanted to herself, ignoring Binnie completely. 'Black Board, Belly Button, Baby's Bum . . . that's it!' she said, with a start. 'Baby's Bum, because it's on a baby's bum – it's to let us know that it's a bum.'

Binnie exploded. 'Baby's arse? You daft cow –

she's not part of a self-assembly kit from Ikea. It might just as well mean Buffalo Bill.'

They started to argue. Hecate intervened, banging her stick on the floor.

'Ladies, ladies, please pull yourselves together. To discover the meaning of the child's mark, we must consult the oracle.'

'Quick, turn the telly on,' said Binnie, looking for the remote control. 'What page is it on, Kate?'

Kate's eye's narrowed. 'You fool, Binnie,' she said. 'I meant that I intend to consult the wise ones, the dark forces, for enlightenment.'

'If you are referring to Mrs Crippin next door then you're out of luck. The nosey old boot has gone to her daughter's caravan in Wales for the week, thank Lucifer,' said Moll.

'I saw her – '

'Enough!' Kate broke in. 'Let's go home, we have work to do.'

That night, they consulted the crystal, they read the Tarot and cast the runes but to no avail. There was nothing for it but for Kate to go into a trance. All was silent as Kate slid deeper and deeper into a trance. Suddenly she spoke: 'Listen well. Remember what I say,' she said, in a Birmingham accent (her spirit guide was from Solihull). 'The mark will foretell the child's future. I see a Blue Balloon . . . and a Bare Breast. Someone is shouting Blonde Bombsite to me . . . and Big Breakfast . . . I see Butlin's, Bognor . . . I hear the strangest tune . . . it goes "blankety blank, blankety blank, blankety blank".'

Suddenly she clutched her throat. Her eyes

widened with fear. 'Bad Blood . . . I see Bad Blood, Born Bad. The child is cursed. I see a man, a small man with facial hear.' Beads of sweat ran down my terrified aunty's forehead. Moll and Binnie were jumping up and down in their seats, desperate to hear who the stranger was.

'Who is he?' they chanted.

'Bobby Ball,' gasped my aunt and fainted.

Of course I was always kept away from the smaller members of Canon and Ball by my mother. She saw to it that our paths never crossed. However, what's written in the stars and on a baby's arse . . .

The ancient art of witchcraft has been practised for centuries. Its secrets have been handed down from generation to generation, from mother to daughter, from auntie to niece. Sometimes when a situation seems impossible, the chips are down and you need a miracle, then a little magic isn't a bad thing – providing you use it wisely.

The most popular request for a spell usually involved attracting true love, my aunts claimed. So here are some powerful love potions from the pages of my aunts' grimoire for you to mull over. Go carefully if you weave a love spell. Be very specific when making your request. Think first – do you really want this person? Are you absolutely 100% certain? Make sure you are, because once the spell is cast then there's no turning back. Never ever use magik to manipulate a person's will. Magical manipulation can have serious consequences with disastrous results.

Cursing is not recommended either. Curses, like chickens, come home to roost, and will return to you threefold – you have been warned! Neither I nor the publishers will accept any responsibility for the consequences. You got that? OK then all you neophyte witches – let's get brewing.

TO MAKE A MAN BURN WITH THE FLAMES OF DESIRE.

You need:
A tall candle about 10 inches in length, either white or lavender
Lavender and musk oil
Paper
A sharp knife
Matches
A candle holder

A love spell should always be performed on a Friday during the waxing phase of the moon. Friday is sacred to Venus, the Goddess of Love.

First take a warm bath, scented with fragrant oils of lavender, rosemary, lily of the valley. Sprinkle rose petals, violets and daisies over the surface of the water. Lie back and have a good, long soak, inhaling steam from the aromatic waters, cleansing the mind as well as the body.

Dry yourself and then go to your bedroom to perform the rite.

It should be tidy and lit by the light of a red (for passion) and pink (for love) candle. Burn incense and joss sticks to help create the perfect mood. You can either work your magic naked, or sky-clad as the witches prefer to say, or you can wear clothes if you wish. Pick something loose and comfortable. If you are going naked then don't forget to draw the curtains! Close the door and make sure that you will not be disturbed. Secrecy is all in witchcraft.

Lie on the bed and anoint the candle with the musk and lavender oil, concentrate on the object of your desire, conjure up erotic visions in your mind of the two of you indulging in a bit of hanky panky! Take your time when doing this as you need to impregnate the candle with your dreams and wishes. Squeeze the candle firmly as you massage the oils into the wax. When you feel that the candle is ready, cut six notches with the knife, making seven separate segments in the candle. Place it securely in the holder and recite the following incantation in a husky seductive voice (it helps if you drink whisky and are a heavy smoker).

You ache to taste my ruby lips
To place your hands upon my hips
This spell I'll whisper in your ear
(Name) you can't resist,
Come here, come here
(Name) come here.

Recite the last part of the spell at least ten times. Write your name on a small piece of white paper, fold it in half and then light it. Take it to the candle and use it to light the wick. When the candle is lit say the following:

May a flame of desire burn in your heart
Your senses awakened by this cupid's dart.

Stare into the flame, visualise your love's face in the centre of it, imagine you're holding a cross-bow, take aim and fire your arrow directly into the flame. The passionate arrow that you have mentally conjured up has scored a direct hit.

Leave the candle to burn down to the first notch. You can lie on your bed and listen to music thinking about your lover, willing him to come to you while this is happening. Extinguish the flame and repeat on seven consecutive nights by which time lover boy will come a' callin' and you will find yourself up those stairs so quickly you wont know what's hit you.

OK, now you've got him, here's how to hang on to him.

TO ENSURE TOTAL FIDELITY IN A MAN AND KEEP HIM FAITHFUL

A powerful but a tricky spell this because the main ingredients are the hairs from a live wolf. No problem if you live in the forest on the Polish/Russian border but it will require a little thought if you live in Widnes. The only place you're gonna find a live wolf is in a zoo. You have two alternatives:

❶ Break in overnight, knock the wolf out by means of a powerful sedative dart, climb over the fence and get your hairs.

❷ Ask the keeper of the wolf enclosure if he will

get you them. Use your feminine wiles to get him to obey your commands, use your witchcraft to make him bow to your will.

Burn the hairs into a powdery ash and sprinkle in the unsuspecting rover's drink. He will never stray again!

MEN

If the wife or girlfriend is a bit of a slapper then grease your private parts with goat's fat before intercourse and she'll never look at another man again. She'll moan about the smell and won't be pleased when she sees the state of the sheets, but she'll be devoted.

WOMEN

If your mate has bewitched you by means of 'the goat fat spell' then the simple antidote to this spell is to pop a live worm in his bedtime Horlicks. This will not only break the spell but will render him impotent. Probably the shock when he finds the worm.

TO ATTRACT A LOVER

If you have no one specific in mind then cast a magical net and see if you can land a whopper. There's plenty of fish in the sea and if you want to land a Prince Charming then this is the spell for you.

On a Friday when the moon is waxing, take some catnip, rosemary and lavender and burn them in fire. If you've got a real coal fire then there's no problem, if you haven't then use your initiative – build a miniature bonfire in the garden or in an ashtray as it only need be tiny. Don't set the house on fire. As the herbs burn recite the following spell.

My true love's face I've yet to see
I know not what his/her name will be
But soon their heart will beat for me
Come hither forth my love
So mote it be.

Within a short time you'll be in the arms of a tasty bit of talent.

BLACK CAT LOVE POTION

This is a very potent love potion. You need to dry and ground in a mortice and pestle the liver of a black cat. Don't kill the moggy! Wait until you come across the poor little corpse of a black cat that has been hit by a car lying in the roadside. Take the liver powder and mix it with some tea leaves in a black teapot. Pour your lover a refreshing and magical cup of tea and watch what happens.

A CHARM TO BRING YOUR LOVER BACK TO YOU

If your man has left you for a younger bit of stuff or your wife has run off with the insurance man then this little charm will bring em running back to the nest.

Stick a needle through the wick of a pink candle if the escapee is a woman or a crimson one if it's a man. Light the candle and, staring at the dancing flame, will your lover to return to you.

Recite the following:
Light of Venus
Light of Love
Burn in (name's) heart
And return to me.

Let the candle burn down. Of course you could always forget about them and get yourself someone new. A change is as good as a rest!

A SPELL TO SILENCE A NOISY NEIGHBOUR

To be performed on the night of a new moon. Light a yellow candle

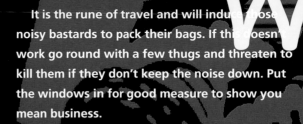

and into a cup of oil (olive, cooking etc.) sprinkle some salt reciting the following words:

Move somewhere far away from me,
Take your music and tv
Your voices raised I'll hear no more
When you have gone and closed the door.

Dip a bird's feather in the oil and draw a rune outside your neighbour's house on the ground. Try to do this without anyone seeing you.

The rune you should draw is this \—\

It is the rune of travel and will induce those noisy bastards to pack their bags. If this doesn't work go round with a few thugs and threaten to kill them if they don't keep the noise down. Put the windows in for good measure to show you mean business.

SPICE UP YOUR BORING SEX LIFE SPELL

If, as Barbara Streisand sang 'Your sex life is boring you to tears after all these years' then this spell will put the spark back into your marriage.

On a Friday night when the moon is full go to your bedroom and light candles to represent sexual love: a pink one for love, a purple one for change and transformation and a yellow one for communication. Burn incense and scatter rose petals on the bed. Take a bath, have a good long soak in fragrant bath oils, dry yourself and return to the bedroom. Play some romantic music (Bert Kampfert is very effective) and standing in front of a mirror wrap a silk scarf around your hips.

Put a mask on, not a joke carnival one, a simple black burglar's mask will suffice. Anoint your chest and throat and stomach with musk oil and repeat the following:

By the flames of Venus
And the passion of Eros
I awaken the flame of desire.

Approach the mirror and raising the palms of your hands in front of you repeat your lover's name three times. You can actually include your old man in this ritual. Get him to lie naked on the bed while you perform the rite. Anoint his body with oils of musk and neroli. He won't need the help of viagra tonight my girl!

WALLACE AND GROMIT

Wallace and Gromit make me vomit. I hate those stupid gozzy-eyed sheep haversacks, unforgivable on anyone over seven. Our Vera bought me a Wallace and Gromit alarm clock for Christmas. When it went off that fellah from Last of the Summer Wine said, 'Come on Gromit, time to get up.' I really enjoyed dancing on that.

WISHING

Take no notice of Mr. Disney's philosophy about wishing upon stars and 'a dream being a wish your heart makes.' A star is a hot gaseous mass that is visible in a clear bright sky as a ball of light and that dream owes more to the cheese on toast you had before you went to bed than your romantic heart sending out signals. It's no good just wishing for things, you have to put a bit of spade work in as well, you know – if you want something then go out and get it. No point dwelling on past failures and regrets. Learn from your mistakes. Instead of saying 'I wish I'd...' say 'Next time I will....'

I wish I'd win the lottery though... I'd probably stand a better chance if I did it.

WORK

Noel Coward said work is more fun than fun, but then he didn't work in the Bird's Eye Factory packing frozen fish fingers nine hours a day did he?

I'd sooner be in work than out of it – if only for the money. What they pay out as dole is ridiculous. I don't know how people can exist.

No matter what you do for a living, unless you're very lucky to be doing a job you love, work is a pain in the arse.

When I was filming a spoof on The Avengers for The Lily Savage Show I spent six hours in full leather tied to a red hot railway track in a siding outside Oxford. It was during that roasting summer and at that moment in time, I'd have given me eye teeth to be packing ice-cold fish fingers in a nice refrigerated factory.

I remember another job I had was on an organic turkey farm. Turkeys get plumper if they are sexually stimulated by hand – honest it's true – and my job was to give 2,000 turkeys a ham shank. It was one of the worst jobs I ever had. On my first day I opened the shed door where the turkeys were kept and was greeted by a dirty great ugly one, its wattle wobbling with indignation. The beast looked me straight in the eye. 'Gobble, gobble,' it said. 'Certainly not!' said I. 'You can have a wank like the rest of them.'

WALKING

My pal Janet Street-Porter is a serious walker. As the Vice President of the Ramblers' Association, there's nothing that our Janet enjoys more than a 20-mile hike across some wild and desolate terrain. I went with her once. I must have been bloody mad. I had to sit down after 200 yards and have a fag. I couldn't keep up with her – she walks too fast. When she told me she was a speed walker I thought she meant she popped a few amphetamines before she went for a hike. I didn't realise that she scorched across the Yorkshire Moors like a bloody roadrunner in the pissing rain. 'Keep up! Keep up!' she screamed at me, taking giant strides across Ilkley Moor as I struggled way behind, my protests for her to slow down falling on deaf ears.

She was also very rude about my choice of clothing and footwear. We ended up having a blazing row on top of the Cow and Calf Rock. 'Wear something warm I said', she screamed at me like Hitler in a kagoule, her glasses all steamed up.

'This is fucking warm', I screamed back, pointing to my beautiful full-length faux leopard fur coat which was by now so heavy from the continuous rain it made even a tiny movement, let alone walking, impossible.

'And when I said "wear boots", I didn't mean thigh-length PVC slappers' boots with a six-inch bleedin' heel.' She went on, 'I meant

sensible walking boots like mine.'

She was wearing a pair of thick woollen men's socks, the tops of which were rolled over, and the most repulsive pair of great clumping clodhoppers she called walking boots. They did nothing for her legs and wild horses wouldn't get me into a pair of them. In fact, I wouldn't be seen dead in any outdoor gear. It's all so unglamorous! Kagoules, anoraks and those awful waxed jackets that stink. Fleecey jackets and tops in the most hideous colours. Purple, red, lilac and brown. Are the manufacturers of outdoor clothing aware that their designers are colour blind sadists with no sense of style whatsoever? The great outdoors and glamour obviously do not go hand in glove. Have you ever seen a hiker with lippy on? Or with a decent shampoo and set? Of course you haven't – a bit of Body Shop Aloe Vera Lip Balm is about as far as they go.

You can stuff this walking lark. Why do you think God invented taxis? I rang one on me mobile and buggered off to Betty's in Ilkley for what Enid Blyton would call a 'slap-up tea'. I left Janet ranting and raving on top of the 'Cow' rock. Very apt, I thought, in the circumstances.

XMAS

Instead of slaving in a hot kitchen making mince pies, brandy butter, Christmas cakes and fancy stuffing, why not buy them from a supermarket? Then you can spend your time enjoying yourself in the pub or at a party.

XMAS PUDDINGS

If your pudding is loaded with coins and thimbles etc., then be sure to tell your guests. One year I forgot to mention it and our Vera ended up in casualty. They found a watch, two holy medals and £2.10s.6d in used change in her stomach.

XMAS SONGS

When Slade's 'So here it is, Merry Christmas' first came out, me and our Vera were always the first up on the dance floor at the work's Christmas 'do'. I thought it was fab. Now, 20 years later, I find that as I'm dragging my poor, tired, battered, parcel-laden carcass around Brent Cross Shopping Centre, and I hear that familiar old tune for the ten millionth time that day, I fuckin' hate it.

YOU'LL NEVER KNOW

A mawkish, sentimental old ballad that was written by Harry Warren and became Alice Fayes' signature tune. It also happens to be one of my favourite songs. Everytime I hear it my eyes fill up.

'You went away and my heart went with you,
I speak your name in my every prayer.
If there is some other way to prove that I love you,
I swear I don't know how
You'll never know if you don't know now.'

They don't write 'em like that anymore. I'm crying as I write, I'm sorry I can't go on. . . .

ZIG AND ZAG

Proof that life exists on other planets.